NO EARTHLY NOTION

NO EARTHLY NOTION

Susan

Dodd

VIKING

VIKING
Viking Penguin Inc., 40 West 23rd Street,
New York, New York 10010, U.S.A.
Penguin Books Ltd, Harmondsworth,
Middlesex, England
Penguin Books Australia Ltd, Ringwood,
Victoria, Australia
Penguin Books Canada Limited, 2801 John Street,
Markham, Ontario, Canada L3R 1B4
Penguin Books (N.Z.) Ltd, 182–190 Wairau Road,
Auckland 10, New Zealand

First published in 1986 by Viking Penguin Inc.
Published simultaneously in Canada

LIBRARY OF CONGRESS CATALOGING IN PUBLICATION DATA
Dodd, Susan, 1946–
No earthly notion.
I. Title.
PS3554.O318N6   1986   813'.54   85–40805
ISBN 0-670-80913-6

Printed in the United States of America by
R. R. Donnelley & Sons Company, Harrisonburg, Virginia
Book design by The Sarabande Press
Set in Janson

For Richard,
Love Abiding

"Where there is great love there are always miracles. Miracles rest not so much upon faces or voices or healing power coming to us from far off, but on our perceptions being made finer, so that for a moment our eyes can see and our ears can hear what there is about us always."

Willa Cather

PART I

Lyman
Gene

*A*s youngsters, Lyman Gene and Murana Bill had often been mistaken for twins, though she was the older by nearly three years. Both were gray-eyed, sandy-haired, and long on teeth, a feature Murana tried to disguise with an uneasy, tight-lipped smile.

Both the Bill children had their father's build: long, heavy bones and sturdy joints without much flesh on them. By the time she was nine, Murana had grown feet so large she could no longer squeeze into her mother's brown-and-white spectator pumps to play dress-up. That Halloween, Murana had made the rounds of Mount Vadalia in a black taffeta cocktail dress...and her brother's high-topped black sneakers. She collected treats in a green satin clutch purse encrusted with gold bugle beads, hoping no one's glance would get as far as her blunt, rubber-tipped toes.

Outfitted as Casey Jones, Lyman Gene mostly shouldered past his sister to stand up front, anyway. At six, he was already as tall as she was. Reaching around him, she timidly proffered her evening bag for Tootsie Pops and Charleston Chews, pressing her rouged lips together in a tight smile of gratitude while her little brother acquainted the neighborhood with the origins of his getup and did earsplitting imitations of a train whistle. "Ain't he a caution, though?" folks said. Murana's dress and bag got little notice, her footwear none.

The following year, Murana persuaded her mother to part with a percale bed sheet and cut stingy eyeholes in it. This costume served for subsequent Halloweens until she was fifteen. Then she outgrew trick or treat. Mama said so. This rite of passage took a load off Murana's mind. Put in charge of the door to her parents' house, she found Halloween better from the giving end.

At twelve, Murana had stopped growing. Everywhere. Just as the other girls in her class were starting to fill out, she stopped. She was already five feet nine inches tall and wore a size ten shoe. Her shoulders and hips were broad, her knees and elbows sharp as weapons. Riding high on her chest were two small points which disappeared altogether in the size twelve her other dimensions called for. Her backside was so meagerly padded that her bones rapped on the wooden pews when she sat down in church—occasionally, worshipers in front would turn around to see why anyone should be knocking at the church door with Mass going on. Verging on womanhood, Murana Bill was the spitting image of her father. But everyone stopped saying so soon enough: it was no compliment, and it was plenty obvious.

Unlike his sister, Lyman Gene grew and grew and grew. And filled out. When he reached his full height—six feet seven inches before his sixteenth birthday—his body seemed to resent its own limitations. Muscles started showing up everywhere. His neck and arms and calves and thighs bulged. There were even hard little ridges along his jaw and under his long, sleepy eyes. Before his knees started showing signs of delicacy in defense of Alben Barkley High, folks said he had a great future in pro football. His senior year, a sportswriter even came from the *Courier-Journal* down in Louisville to do a story about "The Giant of Mt. Vadalia." Murana saved the clipping, laminated by a special machine at the

Savings and Loan, and kept it in her wallet ever after, behind her library card.

Lyman Gene and Murana's parents, Clive and Mary Alice, had married rather late. Clive Bill had been a bachelor confirmed by circumstance. His ingenuity and passion were invested to the hilt in Mount Vadalia Feed and Grain, an enterprise he'd started at the age of eighteen. Aside from graduating high school, a break in family tradition, his proudest achievement was winning, for two consecutive years, the Ralston Purina Company's Regional Good Dealers Award.

Clive had applied himself to trade just as, years before, he'd had to apply himself in Mr. Dundee Hawkins's algebra class. He had a stubborn streak when it came to getting the hang of things, and a long attention span. It was only a matter of time before his Purina sales went over the top. He was rewarded, in 1948, at the Commonwealth Hotel in Lexington, by an all-expense-paid weekend honoring Good Dealers from throughout Kentucky, West Virginia, and Tennessee.

For nearly two months, Clive Bill had been looking forward to this weekend: male companionship, a lively exchange of ideas on customer service, new products, promotional schemes. He'd figured he'd be in his element. So he was heartily disappointed by his first glimpse into the banquet hall. Every fellow in there appeared to have, in addition to a highball glass in his hand, a wife on his arm. It dawned on Clive Bill that he was likely to be a fish out of water here, just like every year in Mount Vadalia when he went by himself to the Rotary Christmas Dinner-Dance. Not only did he lack a wife, he didn't even take a drink.

Clive hung back from the reception table and gazed inside: a city block of red carpet multiplied by mirrors, a blaze of light exaggerated by crystal. At one end of the room, a long head table faced rows of round tables, each draped with the

Purina checkerboard design. Life-size cutouts of domestic pets and farm animals were mounted on the mirrored walls, behind clusters of laughing, loud-voiced Good Dealers and Purina sales reps.

He hesitated, wanting to put off setting foot on this foreign ground. A few feet away, a woman at the baize-covered reception table was smiling at him, her eyes raised momentarily from the blue-and-white adhesive-backed name tags, the pink cardboard stubs, the card file box mottled like black-and-white marble. Her hair, brushed back from her face and falling in loose waves to her shoulders, was chestnut. It glistened like a filly's flank. Her smile hinted at sympathy.

Clive approached the table, straightening his green silk tie. "Hello, my name is—"

The woman laughed, her shoulders shaking a rustle from her black taffeta cocktail dress.

Clive halted midstep, pressing his lips together.

"That's just what the tags say." The woman held one out for him to see. Her fingernails were a dusky rose color and trimmed to a modest oval shape. There was something girlish about her, but she had very womanly hands. "So when you said that, 'Hello, my name is...' I just..."

Clive Bill continued to stare at her hand, taking everything in: her perfect nails, his own name on the tag she held, the narrow platinum band on her fourth finger. Her wedding ring, though he rarely had an eye for such detail, looked exactly like his mother's, and he was taken aback at how it saddened him to see it. He thought again of all the brightly dressed wives across the threshold.

He collected himself. "Why, that's my own name on that card you got there," he said.

"So it is." Pleased complacency made her pretty face even softer. She had dimples.

"But how on earth—"

"Remember we asked you to send a picture?"

He shook his head, thinking of the reservation card he'd had to sign and return to the hotel.

"The regional sales office, Mr. Kemp?" she prompted.

Clive nodded quickly, pretending he'd understood all along.

"Man with a record like yours, we got a regular file on him, like the FBI. Mount Vadalia, Kentucky, right?" The way she pronounced Kentucky, the first part like "kin," gave him a warm, homey feeling.

She rose with a lisping whisper of skirts and leaned over the reception table to fix Clive's name to the lapel of his tan suit. Then, with one motion, she pressed two drink-chits in his palm and gave him a gentle little steer toward the banquet hall. "Y'all have a fine evenin' now, hear?"

He stepped bravely into the bright, noisy room.

Mary Alice Singleton watched Clive Bill for a moment as he made his bashful approach to the disintegrating receiving line. A tall, straight, lonely-looking man, she thought, the sort that needed taking in hand. Her cheeks were flushed. Clive, clapped on the shoulder by her boss, Harrison Kemp, swayed a little. Mary Alice wondered just exactly where Mount Vadalia, Kentucky, might be. A bitty place, surely . . . but maybe one she'd like?

When Mary Alice's husband, Roscoe, had died the previous year in a mining mishap in Muhlenberg County, he'd left his wife free and clear—no mortgage payments and no children. Unfortunately, he'd left no savings account or life insurance policies, either. Mary Alice hadn't even had the funds to hire the lawyer she'd need to bring suit against E. K. Consolidated Coal, whose faulty equipment had widowed her. The company, however, claimed Roscoe Singleton was the faulty one: several of his fellow employees stood ready to testify that Roscoe had been known to drink on the job.

It wasn't true, but the widow was a realist. She'd dropped the idea of a suit, sold the house, and taken her admirable disposition and office skills to Lexington, where she was hired as executive secretary to the regional sales manager of the Ralston Purina Company, to whom she had promptly made herself indispensable.

Turning away from the banquet hall with a vaguely guilty smile, Mary Alice pulled a batch of hand-lettered place cards from her beaded satin bag. She hesitated a moment, a dreamy look in her eyes. Then her practical side reasserted itself and she began to rearrange the cards.

That had been the first year, and Clive would tell anybody who'd listen, years later, that his Good Dealers Award turned out to be the best thing that ever happened to him. His fate seemed to have hinged on feed and grain right from the start, and it frightened him to think back how easily he might have gone into other lines of work, missing the blessings in store for him. "How'd I get so lucky?" he'd ask Mary Alice, a look akin to terror on his face.

"Best not ask life too many hard questions," she'd say, kissing his furrowed brow or the crooked bridge of his nose. "Angel of Mischief'll gitcha."

It had been almost like a movie, that first weekend in Lexington, with Mary Alice sitting behind him at the banquet table in her heaven-blue gown. She told him about her life, and he thought his heart would break with the weight of her past sorrows. But she spoke of them so plainly, laughed so easily. Crystal drop earrings twinkled above her shoulders like tiny chandeliers, and her brave spirit left him speechless with admiration.

When Clive returned to his seat, the bronze plaque with his name on it clutched in his hands, Mary Alice had given him a chaste congratulatory kiss: his first taste of champagne. He very nearly felt like a husband for a moment, the look on her face was so proud. They danced to "Red Sails in the Sunset." Her perfume made his head swim, and he watched how they looked together, whirling across a half-acre of mirror.

The next morning, at the Up-and-At-'Em Farewell Break-fast Buffet, Mary Alice sat beside him again. But she was quieter, less sparkling in daylight. She wore a prim white blouse with a cameo brooch, putting Clive in mind of his mother. Her eyes had a holding-on look in them, and she picked at her eggs and grits and scrapple, didn't touch the fried green apples at all.

Then, right in the middle of her boss's fire-'em-up speechify-ing, she'd leaned over and put her hand on Clive's, right up on top of the tablecloth where anybody could see.

"I wish you wouldn't forget me," she'd whispered.

He'd wanted to kiss her, then and there.

Still a bit dazed, Clive had headed for home. The drive felt like a journey to hopelessness after a panoramic glimpse of all possibility. He was hardly likely to forget her, even if he'd been of a mind to try. He heard her fierce, sad whisper, "I wish you wouldn't..."

I ought to have kissed her, he thought. But he'd missed his chance. Now there was nothing he could do.

Clive was crossing the railroad tracks just outside Mount Vadalia when he noticed the handsome Purina billboard he'd won for his town. It showed a neat little clapboard farmhouse with ruffle-curtained windows, a fine red hulk of a barn loom-ing behind it. A yellow-haired woman scattered chicken feed in the yard. Looking at her, Clive suddenly saw the answer. In fact, he realized he'd known it for all his grown-up days. Clive Bill considered the shape of his life and saw, pure and plain, that it was like a puzzle which, no matter how the problem changed, had only one solution: feed and grain.

The second year wasn't so easy. Mount Vadalia was declin-ing, as the younger people moved away temporarily and forgot to return. That winter the cheese factory went out of business and there were big layoffs in Hazard at the electronics plant that had thrived on war. The previous year's tobacco crop had been poor and was bringing low prices at the burley auctions. Naturally, such reverses were taking a toll on sales of feed and grain and everything else.

But Clive Bill worked with a dreamy desperation. He applied himself to cutting prices and increasing volume and making up the difference by shaving down expenses at the store. When Judy, his bookkeeper-clerk, left to have a baby, Clive took on her work himself, rather than replacing her. He loosened up his credit policies to encourage folks to keep buying. He kept the heat so low in the shop that customers complained of the cold, but he told them the discomfort (and who felt it more than he did?) helped keep the product fresh. At Christmastime, he sent a card to Mary Alice. It had an angel on it. Under the printed message, "Joy to the World," he wrote, "I am not forgetting you."

She did not reply. But on the coldest day of February he got a Valentine. It wasn't signed, but it had an angel, too, and the postmark showed that it came from Lexington.

He needed no more to keep him going. When the final figures were in, Clive Bill was named a Ralston Purina Good Dealer for the second year running. He headed for Lexington with fresh new Kodak prints of his store and his house in his wallet, the tune to "Red Sails in the Sunset" in his head, and his mother's star sapphire engagement ring in his pocket.

He was gone for a week.

When he remembered to come home, he brought a bride along with him.

In Mount Vadalia, Clive Bill's marriage caused quite a stir. He was such a loner, and so bashful, that bachelorhood had seemed his proper station. So when he produced a city bride, and a handsome one at that, folks had to start thinking of him in a different way. This made Clive's neighbors uncomfortable and slightly suspicious—as if he'd betrayed them somehow.

But then the Bills had always been a mite peculiar, being Catholics and all. And this new wife seemed a decent enough sort of person. Right away she started neatening up Clive's house, and she wasn't afraid to get her hands dirty, either. During the busier seasons, she was right there alongside him, helping out at the store.

Mary Alice knew Mount Vadalia wondered about her. She came to her new husband's home prepared to be held at arm's length. It didn't bother her a bit. Folks were welcome to take their time in warming up to her. She meant to do likewise.

In the shadowy, pushed-back part of her mind, Mary Alice admitted vaguely that her first marriage had not been all it should. Roscoe Singleton wasn't a bad man, but he was rough, mule-headed, and not awfully smart. When his wife had come to understand that he would always fall short of her hopes, she'd accepted it. And she would have stayed with him, too, making the best of things. But she had, with his death, faced the shameful fact of her relief. When she buried Roscoe, even as she mourned for the painful and unfair loss of his life, she felt as if she'd been let out of a bad bargain. She meant to do much better this time—for her husband as well as herself. Promising to be Clive Bill's wife, she meant to be his partner in every way. And nobody, nothing, was going to get in the way of that.

Along with making Clive's spare house worthy of a family and learning his business and being a public credit and a private comfort to him, Mary Alice had another project:

As soon as she was settled in, she started traveling to Hazard three times a week, taking instructions to become a Catholic.

The Bills had married in the Church—in the abbreviated, slightly disappointing ceremony allowed for mixed marriages, which made Mary Alice feel like something less than a full partner. But she had given her solemn oath—not only to Clive, but to a priest—that she would become a Catholic wife and mother in as short a time as God and Church rules would allow. This vow was not hard for her. It was what her husband wanted, and she harbored no contrary desires or reservations. Her own people had been Seventh-Day Adventists. Mary Alice had been more than pleased to leave that and just about everything else of her early life behind when she met and married Roscoe Singleton. No one of her family was left, and their stern churchgoing lay in the foggy, distant past, as alien to her now as cow-worshiping Hindus, bowing Moslems, other rites familiar only through hearsay.

The ways of the Roman Catholic Church, at first, seemed every bit as strange. But Mary Alice soon found herself quite smitten with the dignity, the gentleness they conveyed to her. She respected the Mass for its discipline, its reliability—wherever you went, Mass stayed pretty much the same. But above all, she loved it for its privacy. It was not her way, even with God, to wear her heart on her sleeve.

Mary Alice learned to love the Church most of all, though, because her husband loved it so. Clive would emerge onto the sunlit church steps on Sunday mornings with every care gone from his face, every bit of fatigue erased. His eyes shone with love and hopefulness. His wife would look up at him, and seeing the transformation, how could she help but cherish the place, the rituals, that brought him such ease and joy?

Mary Alice took her instructions from Monsignor Jeremiah Shea at St. Boniface parish in Hazard, more than twenty miles from Mount Vadalia. But she didn't mind the time or the driving, the studying or the difficult mysteries. Her eagerness was almost childlike. Even Monsignor Shea regarded her with something close to awe. Her yearning to partake fully in the Sacraments filled the aging, tired priest with admiration and even gratitude. His pastoral duties and routines were touched by a freshess the would-be convert carried into his stuffy office on Monday, Wednesday, and Friday afternoons.

"You needn't rush so," he told Mary Alice gently. "God will still be there when you've finished your lessons."

But he couldn't slow her down. Within less than a year, she was baptized. Clive's friends the McCues, whom Mary Alice barely knew yet, were her godparents. They all, even the monsignor, thought it a rather lovely joke: her godmother was younger than she was.

In a few more weeks, Mary Alice made her First Confession. She received First Communion on a June Sunday, and afterward, in a private ceremony in the rectory, Clive and Mary Alice renewed their wedding vows. "Just a little extra precaution," Monsignor Shea said, winking at Mary Alice. The McCues, the only invited guests, produced a bottle of champagne and a handful of rice. For the rest of their lives, Clive and Mary Alice Bill celebrated their anniversary on the tenth of June, rather than in April, when they'd actually been married.

The birth of Murana Bill the following year was regarded as a minor miracle. No one, least of all the principals, guessed Clive and Mary Alice would produce a child so promptly at their age. Even Murana, from the first, seemed to regard the world as something she never expected to see. She slipped from the womb with barely a peep, and as she grew, acquiring the nuances of speech and motion, her personality remained cautious. She was an even-tempered, unassuming child.

If Murana's appearance was a minor miracle, Lyman Gene's was a major event. He entered the world backwards and boisterous and already overgrown, putting an end to his mother's childbearing years once and for all. The delivery aged Mary Alice, but she never minded: what she lost in elasticity and luster was more than compensated by what she gained in joy. And Clive, after the boy's birth, was more infatuated with his wife than ever. The children, especially his son, produced in him the glad astonishment of a man who, having given up all hope of singularity, suddenly finds himself the center of a child's universe.

In fact, Clive never quite got over his amazement at having won a wife. As his son and daughter grew, he wooed their mother more ardently. Her cooking and housekeeping and childrearing seemed to him both tender and erotic. A soul of hoarded passions, he squandered them on his small family without reserve.

In December of 1967, as Clive and Mary Alice Bill were returning from the Rotary Christmas Dinner-Dance, their week-old Plymouth Belvedere sedan stalled on the railroad tracks in the path of an oncoming L & N freight. Both were killed outright.

Clive never saw what hit him. He'd been looking with stricken eyes at the old Purina billboard, faded and dim. The farmhouse and barn were peeling away, and the woman looked disreputable as she fed her scrawny flock. Where had the time gone?

As always, when her husband experienced a moment of doubt, Mary Alice had been squeezing his hand.

Lyman Gene Bill had just passed his fifteenth birthday and reached his full height when his parents died. His sister, not quite eighteen, set out to be a mother to him with a dim, dark uneasiness at the back of her mind. She'd wanted her brother to herself all along.

Murana tried not to think a passing wish could have prompted the Angel of Mischief to stoke up the locomotive, muffle its whistle, tamper with wires under the hood of her father's new car. For months after her parents died, though, she dreamed their eyes flickering around her bed, pleading with her from the darkness to reconsider her longings.

Now Lyman Gene was hers alone, and all she had. And doing for him shielded her from the guilt and horror. Like her mother, Murana believed it best not to ask life too many questions. Her baby brother, despite his size and strength, depended on her now. It had been left to her to finish his rearing, and if she lacked her father's passion, she had at least his constancy. And her mother's cheerfulness. Above all, however, Murana Bill inherited her parents' conviction that Lyman Gene was a miracle and a gift from God.

2

*T*he town of Mount Vadalia, which often produced unanimous opinions, would have felt a good mite better about the Bill children had Clive and Mary Alice only left kin. Anywhere, even in California—why, a third cousin twice-removed in New York City would have been better than nobody at all. Sturdy and commonsensical as she was, the girl hadn't been out of school but six months. It hardly seemed right for her to take full charge of that bear-pawed baby brother of hers. Lyman Gene was a regular handful.

But Murana told everybody who asked—and sooner or later, everybody did, even Preacher Motley from Calvary Hill Third Baptist Church had paid her a call—that she wouldn't have it any other way. And without disclosing anything too confidential, Mr. L. T. Moody of the Calhoun Savings and Loan eased folks' minds some by letting it be known that the Bill children were right well off.

Besides the house, the feed and grain store, and a substantial insurance policy, Clive had collected small parcels of land over the years. Mary Alice had made it her business to find the proper sort of tenants for these properties. In fact, it had been the proceeds from the sale of her first husband's house that had financed the ventures. Funny, she was so pert and comely, nobody'd ever given much thought to her cunning. Her reputation as one smart cookie was bestowed posthumously. In no time at all, people forgot they hadn't always thought of her that way. It became unanimous.

Between their mother's practicality and their father's passion, Murana and Lyman Gene were left well-fixed. The sturdy yellow house on River Street, which Clive had occupied since before his marriage, was bought and paid for and tight as a drum.

Profligate with flowered chintz and needlepoint, hooked rugs and patterned wallpaper, Mary Alice Bill had lavished each room with her attentions. She favored extravagant Victorian furniture: sideboards and chiffoniers with carved scrollwork and clawed feet, tables with cool slabs of marble and inscrutable puzzles of Chinese inlay. Each commode and candlestand seemed to her a prize: won for her at an auction, refinished by her husband with infinite patience. Both Clive and Mary Alice had known deprivation. Each had expected to wind up alone. But their dreams had come through unscathed, and their home now conformed to those long-tended dreams; it was a perfect talisman of domestic romance. Morning glories climbed trellises on the kitchen walls. By sunlight or lamplight, the parlor gleamed like a ruby.

When the children were young and unruly, Clive had paneled the basement in knotty pine and called it the Rumpus Room . . . later, the Ruckus Room. It had its own bathroom with wallpaper in a nautical design and a bar at one end with four long-legged stools. Neither Mary Alice nor Clive had much taste for drink. The shelves behind the bar were stocked with seltzer, chocolate and strawberry syrups, nuts, candied cherries and homemade root beer. A milk-shake machine, just like in a real soda fountain, stood beside a yellow-domed popcorn maker. Across the room, facing a daybed and two Naugahyde recliner chairs, a honey-colored console, six feet long, held a television and a high-fidelity record player. Clive's collection of antique farming implements hung from nails on the pine walls.

The night after his parents died, Lyman Gene had started sleeping in the basement. He didn't notify his sister of the change—she knew it well enough. He simply went down to the Ruckus Room and made up the daybed with some sheets he found in the clothes dryer.

Murana, of course, was occupied with callers that evening, running from parlor to kitchen, serving coffee and cake. Passing by the basement door, she'd hear the television, but she didn't call down to Lyman Gene when new visitors arrived. If he wanted to see folks, he'd be up. If not, she wouldn't interfere. The boy was too young for all this tragedy anyway. The calling hours at Fern Brothers' were to be the next day, the funeral the morning after that. If she could have spared her brother the social amenities of mourning, she would have. But that simply wouldn't be right.

Mr. Riley McCue and his wife Glenda had offered to see to arrangements, and Murana was grateful. She didn't trust herself to manage such things properly.

Glenda McCue, a frugally built woman inclined to jumpy movements and nervous laughter, had been in and out of the Bills' house all day. By late afternoon, her overbleached hair was nearly standing on end and there were deep lines around her mouth. She could hardly look at Murana without her eyes filling.

Around five o'clock, the telephone rang for what seemed like the hundredth time. Glenda, sitting at the dining room table with the girl, sprang up as if she were on fire. "Let me," she said. "Must be Rile." Her husband had left nearly two hours earlier to go to the funeral home.

Glenda spoke into the kitchen phone in a voice too low for Murana to hear. When she returned, she was even paler than she'd been before and she kept her eyes on the carpet.

"What about clothes?" she said.

"Reckon I can wear Mama's black wool suit," Murana answered absently.

"No, honey, I meant..."

The girl was gazing out the window into the yard. Winter made everything look so mean-spirited, she thought, like nothing beautiful would ever befall the earth again. The creek was paralyzed with ice. The sky was already dark, inky clouds piled on top of the western hills, where the remnants of a sunset might have been.

"Murana?" Glenda McCue's voice was soft and tentative, and when Murana turned from the window, she found that the woman was weeping again. "It's clothes for your mama and daddy, I meant. They need to know... down to the funeral home."

"Oh." Murana got up and walked through the kitchen door.

Glenda waited five minutes. Then she followed the girl out to the kitchen, fully expecting to see her collapsed, in tears. But she was standing at the sink, washing dishes. Her face was composed, her eyes dry.

Glenda picked up a tea towel and began wiping the silverware. "I hate to be bothering you with it, honey," she said. "But it's not a thing that can wait."

"It's hard to think about, is all," Murana said.

"Sure. Sure it is."

"Seems like I'm just having trouble paying attention."

"Maybe Lyman Gene—"

"No." The girl's whisper was horrified.

The heavy silence in the overheated kitchen was interrupted by the buzzing of the oven timer. Murana removed a large tube pan from the oven and the fragrance of cinnamon filled the room.

"Maybe you'd best leave it to me?" Glenda said.

Murana thought of this woman, hardly more than a stranger, moving around in her parents' bedroom, picking through the closet and dresser drawers, touching Pa and Mama's most personal things, choosing the clothes they'd wear for all eternity. The idea seemed shameful, unbearable. But when she tried to imagine seeing to it herself, Murana sickened. She heard the screams of anguish she was keeping locked so securely inside herself, and she knew that if she let them out even once, they would fill the world and she would never, never be able to push them back inside again. Glenda was no stranger, she told herself. She and Riley were the closest thing to friends Mama and Pa ever had. Besides, the caskets were going to be closed. Clothing didn't hardly matter.

"If you don't mind," Murana said.

Glenda patted her arm.

"Only . . . Mama was partial to blue."

"Reckon I'll just go on up, then," Glenda said.

Murana nodded, pressing her lips together, as she started loosening the edges of the coffee cake from the sides of the pan with a bread knife. "Thank you kindly," she said.

That night, moving through a gentling mist of sorrow, Murana greeted a steady stream of visitors. By nine-thirty, the parlor cleared out. She opened the door to the basement wider to listen to the sound of the TV as she washed up cups and saucers and cake plates. Twice Lyman Gene laughed hoarsely, and Murana shivered. He hasn't really taken it in yet, she thought. God help us when the time comes...

At half-past ten, she went upstairs to get ready for bed. She moved around her yellow bedroom barefoot and on tiptoe, hoping to hear her brother coming up from the basement. She wet her hair over the bathroom sink and wound it on spool rollers. She turned down her bed. Finally, when she was just about to go down and look in on him, the stairs creaked.

When he saw her waiting above him on the landing, her head swathed in pink netting, Lyman Gene smiled absently. Then he went past her into his room, pulled the pillow out from under the bedspread, and started back down the stairs.

"Reckon I'll turn in," he said.

Murana picked at the smocked yoke of her flannel night-gown and said nothing.

From that night on, Lyman Gene slept in the cellar, tucked in amid mementoes of old farms and ice-cream socials and his parents' untold dreams.

Murana felt bereft, especially at first, having the whole second floor to herself. Bit by bit, day after day, Lyman moved his things downstairs until nothing was left in his room but the bed and what he'd outgrown: some tattered clothing, his Lionel trains, a shoebox full of Tinkertoys, and a pair of high-topped black sneakers. She put the sneakers in her own closet and left the rest be.

In the days following the funeral, this dim damp lower room drew both the Bill children. The soda fountain, the cluttered walls, Artie Shaw records and the little saloon lamp that twirled rainbows on the ceiling... the chilly basement revealed the secret life of Clive and Mary Alice, the frivolity only their offspring knew, and now it consoled them. Their mother had danced the blackbottom; their father had played the spoons.

Murana sat on the daybed, lackadaisically cross-stitching a dresser scarf. Lyman Gene was removing scythes and horse-shoes and oak-handled hatchets from their nails, handling them like holy relics. They hadn't been touched in years.

The boy seemed to have inherited a birthright of passion and patience overnight. Quiet and devoted as an acolyte, he polished the dark rusted blades, oiled their wood fittings. Every few minutes his sister stole an uneasy glance at him. There was something very fragile about his concentration, as if the slightest distraction might be shattering. He was refusing to eat, and his huge frame had begun to look gaunt.

Tiring of her needlework, Murana got up and started dusting the heavy glass banana split dishes behind the bar. The chore was unimportant, merely an excuse to stay in the cellar, where she could keep an eye on Lyman Gene. Suddenly, her attention was drawn to the milk-shake machine. Its chrome-

and-green-enamel shape cast a shadow like a charmed cobra against the wall. Inspired, she ran upstairs and slipped out the back door, returning shortly with ice cream, bananas, and an extra half-gallon of milk.

While Lyman Gene was off looking for a tube of epoxy, Murana quickly cracked two eggs into the stainless-steel beaker. By the time her brother came back down the stairs, she was scooping thick clots of Hershey's syrup from a jar with a long-handled spoon.

The machine whirred, fitfully at first, then smoothly. Murana poured a dense, slightly lumpy beige mixture into a tall, shapely glass and set it on the bar.

"Come here, Bubba."

"Busy," Lyman Gene said mildly, not looking up.

Murana sighed.

Lyman Gene applied himself to a splintered fragment of veneer. His great head hung low, his nose very near the nozzle of the tube of glue.

"Ain't sniffin' that stuff, are you?"

"Leave a body be, Murana," he said in a warning tone.

She picked up the milk shake and carried it to the table where her brother was working. "Now you listen here."

"CrimineyCHRIST!"

"And there won't be no profanity in this house, neither."

Lyman Gene grunted.

"Wouldn't talk that way if Mama was here." Her tense face grew lax with hopeless love. "I made you something. Bubba. Please?"

The flat of his mammoth hand slammed down, striking the tube of glue. It split at the seam and a clear ooze spread on the tabletop and between his fingers.

"Jumping Jesus, will you look what you done!"

"I'm sorry," Murana said.

Then they both began to cry.

Murana wept softly, easily. It was more than three weeks

since what remained of her parents had been laid in the ground on a half-frozen hillside outside of town. Sometime between then and now, Christmas had come and gone. She'd courteously answered the questions of a priest, a lawyer, a man from the bank, a woman from county welfare, and a host of neighbors and friends. Generally, she'd held up right well. But in between times, Murana had done a good bit of crying. So tears came effortlessly now, and felt natural—like the continuation of a long conversation, occasionally interrupted.

Lyman Gene's grieving was different, though. Foreign and terrible and violent, it seemed bent on tearing his huge frame apart. Frightened by the depth of her brother's sorrow, Murana eased one step back from him.

Lyman Gene covered his face with his hands. A drop of glue glistened in his eyebrow. Murana moved closer again, putting her fingers around his wrist to move his hand away from his eye. He lowered his head farther, hiding his face.

"Oh, God damn it to Jesus shit Christ hell!"

It was the sum total of his vocabulary for evil, Murana thought. With the awful words out of the way, she no longer feared the great raging boy. Still weeping, she leaned over and gathered him in her arms. Like a baby. But his weight unbalanced her. She fell onto the arm of his chair. His arm came up to steady her there.

They held each other for a very long time. The girl's crying was nearly silent, a mourning of held breath and loosed tears. It might have gone on forever. But her brother's sobbing was loud and dry, exhausting.

Finally, it wore them both out. They grew still. With one bony arm clinging to Lyman's massive neck, Murana reached for the glass on the table.

The ice cream had melted, leaving the milk shake thin, with bits of banana pulp floating on top like the scum on a pond. Murana stirred it with her finger before holding the glass to her brother's lips.

He looked at her warily.

"Come on now," she said, putting her finger in her mouth. "Sweet."

Lyman Gene squeezed his eyes shut. He sighed. Then he took a gulp.

"That's my boy. My Bubba."

Pretending to sip from the glass herself every once in a while, she got the milk shake down him. It was the first nourishment the boy had taken in weeks. When the glass was finally empty, there was a milky mustache on his upper lip and a hard, jewel-like droplet on his left eyebrow. He looked childlike and very beautiful.

"At least we got each other," she said.

Lyman Gene did not reply. He'd fallen asleep.

Murana remained half-slumped on the arm of his chair. Her shoulder was pinned behind his neck and both her feet, dangling above the floor, had gone numb. Concentrating on the rainbows on the ceiling, she took the smallest breaths she could, hanging on, silently, waiting for her brother to come back.

When a full month had gone by, and Lyman Gene was drinking milk shakes regularly and even taking some solid food, Murana set her mind to getting him back to business. And most especially, to school.

On a freezing Monday morning in mid-January, she put on her mother's lilac chenille wrapper. She brushed out her hair and washed her face, before descending to the pitch-black basement. It was six-forty-five. She meant to rouse her brother in no uncertain terms.

She felt her way down the steep stairs without turning on the lights, her fingers brushing the wainscoting as if it were braille. The air smelled musty and faintly like oil.

"Bubba?"

"Leave me be," he muttered, pressing his face into the pillow. "Git offa me."

"Not on your life. Time for school." She switched on a small lamp. Then, tentatively, she began poking him.

Emerging from sleep, the huge boy resisted. Every ounce of his hard, hulking body and every corner of his stubborn soul fought off his sister's hands. His eyes squeezed shut. His meaty fingers curled in fists. His arms and legs stiffened. But worst of all, he refused to talk to her. His full lips drew into a tight line across his awesome set of teeth.

Murana tried everything she could think of. She reasoned and pleaded and threatened. She offered bribes. She tried to shake his unmovable shoulder and tugged on his hair. But she might as well have been taunting and tweaking a monument.

When he didn't move a muscle, she put on every single light, then the TV, too, full-blast. The face of Hugh Downs appeared on the screen, but his voice, even at top volume, lacked authority. Murana returned to the daybed, stripped back the pile of covers, and started tickling the soles of her brother's feet.

Lyman Gene was ticklish. It was the one weakness his sister had been able to exploit as a child. But it didn't work now. His eyes still shut, Lyman flexed one bulging leg and sent her careening across the cold basement floor with his heel.

For the first time in her life, Murana really fought him. Getting a running start from the bar, she hurled herself on his obstinate form, pounding his chest and shoulders. Her own ferociousness amazed her. As he pushed her face roughly away, she sank her own not inconsequential teeth into his wrist.

That opened his eyes. "Well, you damn she-devil whore," he said. His voice was gruff with sleep, but more surprised than angry.

Where had he learned such talk? Murana had a hand raised

to slap him good when she saw the blood that was trickling down his arm.

Lyman Gene saw it, too. Suddenly, he seemed smaller. Almost frail. He looked from his torn wrist to his sister's stricken eyes and smiled uncertainly. And Murana felt more horrified than when she'd opened the front door expecting Pa and Mama, only to find the grim-faced constables looking at her.

An hour later, smiling and neatly dressed, Lyman Gene left for school. An elaborate bandage on his wrist was concealed by the cuff of his Alben Barkley athletic jacket.

Murana stayed in the house all day, wearing her mother's old robe. She wept, as she went about fixing her brother's favorite dinner: chicken and dumplings, fried okra, Waldorf salad, and lemon meringue pie. Her feet moved cautiously over the gleaming linoleum, as if the floor might crumble away beneath them.

By midafternoon, her fits of weeping finally subsided. Things started coming clear. And it seemed to Murana then that she had been woefully mistaken. There wouldn't be any more trouble about Bubba going to school, she knew, but other things would need settling. Her brother was almost a man, and men were a mystery to her. Whatever had made her think she'd be able to see to him?

She fiercely beat a bowl of egg whites by hand, recollecting how easily blood had spurted from the boy's tough skin. He'd already apologized, and even hugged her, before he left. But Murana didn't know how she'd ever be able to forgive herself.

They never came to blows again, perhaps because they both understood she really couldn't bear it. It was true that Lyman was a near-man, a near-mystery. But Murana had overlooked one thing: while she meant to take care of him, he meant to take care of her. Devotion filled the gap between their perceptions. It was enough to get them by.

Lyman Gene used his sister's love to good advantage, setting his heart on meeting her hopes. An indifferent student, he made better grades after his parents were gone than he'd ever made before.

Religion seemed slightly foolish to him. Even as a youngster, Lyman had felt a certain disdain for the idea of sitting passively in a dim church and expecting God to sit up and take notice of such a useless thing. He believed in God, all right, but he saw Him as a foreman of a great factory, a warrior, a graceful and mighty athlete Whose power lay in stride and reach, heft and rage.

But the boy would never tell his sister this, any more than he would have repudiated his parents' version of God and worship by laughing in their trusting, lovestruck faces.

Murana had never learned to drive. After the accident (which seemed to him proof positive of God's brute strength) Lyman Gene was the one who drove the twenty miles to Mass each Sunday. Afterward, he'd take Murana to the Pancake House for breakfast. He would always treat, even though the money all came from the same place and he and his sister both knew it.

During his last two years of high school, Lyman Gene outgrew his awkwardness. More stamina and raw courage than superior skill, great speed, or true grace, his athletic ability nonetheless brought him a good deal of attention. As a younger boy, he'd seemed somewhat freakish, the size of him. Now, however, he became a figure of respect. His prowess and good nature were enhanced by the terrible end of his parents and his devotion to his homely sister. He tapped a tenderness in girls and women that raised certain opportunities for misadventure. Lyman let most of these pass him by. And those he simply couldn't resist he took great pains to conceal. He arranged for the coach's wife to bring Murana to his football games, and he always saw her home himself—even if there was a party afterward.

Murana cherished her brother's attentions. He bought her

flowers every Mother's Day, even though there were flowers blooming for free in the yard.

In June of 1970, Lyman Gene Bill graduated from Alben Barkley High. His commencement was the proudest moment of his sister's life. Although his grades put him only just in the middle of his class, he was unanimously elected by his classmates to receive the Barkley Award, an ornate silver trophy with his name engraved between two figures Murana made out as either angels or gods.

When Lyman was called up to the auditorium stage, he was given a standing ovation. Shyly, he approached the microphone and shook hands with the principal, Mr. Jenks. Suddenly, he seemed very little like a man, despite his height and breadth and new blue business suit. All the awkwardness, so recently shed, came over him again. When he opened his mouth and tried to speak, a ragged breathy noise was amplified through the packed hall. The boy grinned nervously, exposing his extraordinary teeth.

"I thank y'all . . . a honor I surely don't deserve."

In the eighth row, between the coach's wife and Riley McCue, Murana felt a terrible constriction around her heart. She stopped breathing.

Lyman Gene lowered his head, and a lock of hair looped above his right eye. There wasn't a sound in the hot auditorium except the low hum of the PA system.

Finally, he raised his eyes to search through the audience. When he found Murana, he smiled. Furtively, one of her hands rose from her lap, ready to help him along, to hold him up.

"I'll be pleased to accept this thing, though . . . long as nobody objects I'll be giving it to my big sister."

On a sea of hands and faces, Murana was washed up beside him on the stage, feeling helpless and very small. The whole town was there, on its feet, cheering, stamping. Murana's eyes flew up to the raftered ceiling for a moment. The din seemed bound to make it fall. Why, he could be the governor, Murana thought. Even the president, maybe. Only then he wouldn't be hers anymore.

Sensing her alarm, Lyman Gene threw back his head and laughed. With his laughter, the cheering grew louder, the microphone shrieked. He pushed her to the edge of the stage for a bow.

Then Murana Bill disappeared again, obliterated by her baby brother's immense embrace. There wasn't a dry eye in the house.

The silver trophy was placed on top of the piano in the parlor, flanked by Clive Bill's Good Dealer Awards. After she put it there, Murana couldn't stop going over to touch it. She started keeping a square of flannel in the piano bench so that each time she pressed her fingers to the silver cup, she could wipe her prints off. Lyman Gene's graduation was the one sublime achievement of her life.

But her sorriest defeat came a scant week later: her brother told her his mind was made up, he was joining the army.

They sat on the front stoop. It was the supper hour and River Street was ghostly quiet in the listless light. The air was heavy with a brewing storm. Murana watched the clouds seething on the other side of the mountains. Soon they'd be sliding over the green slopes, pushing thunder ahead of them. She reminded herself to shut the upstairs windows before they sat down to eat.

"I got to, Sissy," Lyman Gene said.

"You got to go to college is what you got to do." But a forecast of defeat was already in her voice. "What about the scholarship at Murray State? The football?"

"Take me noplace."

"What are you talking about, boy? The award and..."

"I'm a big boy in a bitty town, is all."

"Bubba, you're—"

"I'm goin' in the army. Time I growed up and got movin', while I still got knees holdin' me up."

Murana was sitting very close to him, but she kept her face turned away. Back behind the house, the Rushing Milk River, swollen with spring rain, sloshed up its banks. Murana wondered if there mightn't be a flood with one more storm. There never had been real floods in these parts, so far as she knew. First time for everything, she thought.

"I never was good at school," Lyman Gene said, trying to appease her. "The decent marks was a kindness, mostly."

"You tried real hard," Murana said.

"And now I'm tryin' to grow up."

"Pa and Mama—"

"Wouldn't ask for more," he finished for her.

His sister, crushed, heard the truth in the words. "I'll be scared to death the whole time, Bubba."

"Yeah. Me, too, I reckon."

She turned. Her face was pale and slightly translucent, like the white of a soft-boiled egg. His heart lurched, but his will held steady.

The following week, Murana watched her brother board a bus for Fort Knox. There was no gentling mist to blur her grief this time. She saw the bus in sharp relief against the vivid hills long after it was good and gone.

*I*t turned out to be a painfully hot, dry summer. The days were stupefying, the nights a misery. On Saturdays, the farmers came to town and sat silently in the tavern or at the soda fountain in the pharmacy. They claimed patches of shade outside the general store and the Dairy Queen.

Crops were ruined. Livestock was decimated. By August wells were running dry. Men didn't speak of their misfortunes. They glanced away from each other, their eyes hollowed out by shame, their mouths bitter. In the stores, their wives and children moved hopelessly among displays of things they could no longer afford, barely whispering their essential wants.

In July, the feed and grain store, started by Clive Bill more than thirty-five years before, had gone bust. Mr. Tommy Tate, who'd given Murana and Lyman Gene fair price for it, moved his family to Paducah, where his wife's people could put them up until he got back on his feet.

Without Lyman Gene to do for, Murana had no idea just what she was meant to do. Taking care of her brother was the only job she was qualified for. Well, she'd done pretty well in the bookkeeping class she'd taken in high school, but there were no jobs anyway. She knew she ought to be grateful. Mr. Moody at the bank assured her she'd never have to work, provided she took reasonable care. But Murana felt like one of those laid off, left destitute and humbled by her uselessness.

As long as she'd had Lyman Gene to see to, it hadn't occurred to her to prod the future or probe the past; she kept them under wraps. Now, however, the present seemed a total loss. She had counted on her brother's appetite, his outgrown clothes, his vitality and ungainly needs to outline her days for her.

Throughout that parched summer, Murana didn't feel the heat. While the town seemed to shrivel and wilt around her, there was gooseflesh on her arms. In the evenings, when her neighbors sat on their porches fanning themselves and eating ice cream and cool salads, Murana huddled over the kitchen table sipping cups of hot broth. She knew that before the heat wave broke her baby brother would get orders to go to war, and the chill of his grave was settling in her bones.

Murana had taken up needlework. Sewing had been one of Mama's glories, a skill that had seemed to have magic in it. Mary Alice had made all of their clothes, her own and the children's, and near everything for the house—curtains and tablecloths, pillow shams and ruffled skirts for whatever could comfortably wear one. Her stitching, all done by hand, was as fine, Pa said, as gnat tracks.

Mary Alice had insisted that her daughter learn to use a needle. It was one of those things a girl needed to get by in this world, she claimed. But it was clear from the start that Murana didn't have the magic in her fingers, and never would. Her hands were too large, too clumsy. Little by little, the girl had taken over the kitchen instead, freeing her mother to stay in the sunny sewing room upstairs, humming torch songs as her quicksilver pinking shears fashioned adornments from scraps and hand-me-downs.

The sewing room had been left untouched, its door shut, since Mama'd been gone. Desperate to be useful, however, to keep her hands occupied as her mind raced after her brother in the Asian jungle, Murana was finally driven to her mother's workbasket. The house was growing tatty. Things needed mending, replacing. Besides, the sewing room window looked right out over the front walk, a bird's-eye view for the mailman's daily stop.

One winter day, when the necessary repairs to the household linens were nearly completed, Murana opened a small sea captain's chest looking for a darning egg. Inside she found a half-finished quilt. The piecing was already done. The batting and backing were basted in place. But only at the very center had the quilting itself been started.

When Murana unrolled the quilt, a sheaf of tissue pattern pieces fluttered to the floor at her feet, and among them, a sheet of coral writing paper with a scalloped edge. On it, in Mama's round hand, were the instructions. It was named the Hosanna Quilt, for the shapes of palm leaves which had been waved in honor of Jesus when He went riding into the golden city of Jerusalem on a donkey.

Murana studied the quilt. Spread out, it covered the whole floor of the little room, an intricate pattern of bright- and soft-colored squares that dazzled her eyes. Each square had four smaller squares inside, and those were made of triangles that formed the palm leaves.

The more Murana tried to figure out the complicated design, the less clear it seemed to her. Just as she'd begin to understand the parts, the whole would take over and confound her. But after a while, she began to recognize old familiar things in the maze: swatches of her own childhood dresses, Mama's favorite frocks, Pa's once-best ties. Then she noticed, strewn here and there like emeralds, bits of the elegant evening bag which had, in Vadalia, been good for nothing grander than trick-or-treat nights. Gold beads winked on the scraps of green satin like tiny stars, very far away.

Murana wondered if Mama mightn't have mourned some, cutting jagged scissor blades into lovely and dear old things that had outlived their uses. But no, Mama had never been much given to mourning or regret. She must have been gladdened by the new beauty she was putting together, secretively, in her small ivy-papered room.

Murana sat on the gold velveteen settee by the window and gathered up the quilt. So awfully tiny, those careful stitches of Mama's. So even. As she studied her mother's handiwork, it seemed to Murana that she held the whole happy history of her family, her very life, in her lap. For a time, she even forgot to keep an eye out for the postman.

But eventually she remembered. She went downstairs to wait for him, taking the unfinished quilt with her. Her hands would never, she knew, be as graceful and delicate as Mama's. Never as sure. But she would finish her mother's work, and respectably, decently. Even if she had to rip the stitches out over and over again. Even if it took her years. The Hosanna Quilt would give her something to hold on to as she waited for Bubba to come home.

She worked on the quilt a little bit each day for as long as her brother was away. Gradually, her stitching improved. In fact, it seemed to help steady her hands in the excruciating hour before the mail was dropped through the brass slot in the front door.

Once a week, faithfully, Lyman Gene wrote to her. His letters were full of brash pride. He'd been sent to Fort Polk, where they had "a play jungle," he said, for special training. He looked to coming battle like a championship football game. He was learning all the plays. Growing tough and lean. He sent her his dash and bravado like extravagant presents.

At the end of basic training, he also sent a photograph. He was in dress uniform, with nearly all his hair cut off. Below his shiny billed cap, pink swaths of bare scalp skirted his ears. His face was thinner, his forehead creased, his eyebrows bleached by the Louisiana sun. With an American flag behind him, a world globe at his right elbow, he looked a perfect hero.

In a letter, however, Lyman Gene said how he'd had no

pants on when the photograph was taken. The jacket and cap were briefly borrowed, like a costume. No pants: he made it into a great joke, describing how foolish he felt, half-naked before a camera with his friends watching, waiting their turns. Murana had to smile over his letter, but she wished he hadn't told her. She could never look at the picture without seeing past its lower edge to the mottled rose and cream skin of her brother's thighs, without wondering were his boxer shorts soiled or torn. At night she dreamed of him being chased through the jungle by eyeless savages, his naked legs shredded by thorny vines. Bullets swooped around his head like bats.

The heat carried over into October, and Private Lyman Gene Bill came home on a weekend pass.

When the Greyhound bus pulled in, Murana was waiting across the street under the tattered awning Tommy Tate had left to flap above the boarded-up front of the feed and grain store. She was wearing a mint-green piqué dress with a large straw hat and her best white kid shoes, the same outfit she'd worn to Bubba's graduation.

At first, she hardly knew him, so slim and straight and dignified in his uniform. Kitty-corner from where Murana stood, before the plate-glass window of Ford's Pharmacy, a dozen or more of Lyman Gene's friends had turned out to welcome him. The girls, like Murana, wore summer dresses.

When Lyman stepped down from the bus, a cheer went up. He stopped in the middle of the intersection. An olive drab duffel bag hung from his shoulder, and he carried his cap in his hand. He looked toward the pharmacy, at the girls. Then he turned and looked at the feed and grain store.

For a moment, he stood stock-still. Then, his teeth bared in a great grin, he bounded across the dusty street to his sister.

His bag and cap fell to the curb as he lifted her up and swung her in a giddy arc. One of her white pumps flew into the street. He growled playfully and shook her, like a puppy with an old sock.

"Bubba. Oh, Bubba."

She saw that he really hadn't changed a bit.

He belonged to Murana again for less than forty-eight hours, two blissful days she could scarcely remember afterward.

She'd been cooking for a week before his visit, but when she got him home, all she could think to do was cook some more. On Saturday night half the town came by, packing the house and spilling out onto the porch. There was plenty of food for everybody.

"We're proud of you, boy—*proud!*" the men told him, slipping five-dollar bills into his uniform pockets and toasting his health and heroism from half-pint bottles in the alley behind the garage. Moonlight turned the sweat on their foreheads and the stubble on their chins to silver.

Lyman Gene hooted and goose-stepped across the wet grass, slightly tipsy. He addressed everyone, even his sister, as "Sir." The wives and daughters of the men who egged him on followed his antics with moist, covetous eyes. The young people danced in the Ruckus Room, dusting off Clive's old records. They turned out all the lights except for the one that tossed rainbows up to the ceiling, and "Red Sails in the Sunset" wafted through the open windows of the house and down the street.

At two-thirty in the morning, the house a shambles, Lyman stumbled off to bed. When Murana went to look in on him later, she found him in his old bedroom upstairs. He was laughing in his sleep, smears of a dozen different shades of lipstick on his mouth and neck and ears. He would have been stark naked, but for the billed cap that covered him like an overgrown fig leaf.

On Saturday afternoon, Lyman had called on Dunfey Jones, the lawyer who managed the Bill family's affairs. Murana knew her brother was having a will drawn up, but she wouldn't tolerate him discussing it with her.

On Sunday morning, after the nine o'clock Mass in Hazard,

he took her to the Pancake House. It was crowded, the air thick with melted butter and bacon grease. As they waited for the waitress to bring their waffles, Lyman Gene leaned across the table and took his sister's hand. "If something happens to me," he said.

Murana pulled away and clapped her hands over her ears.

"I'm not saying it's gonna. Just—"

"Don't, Bubba. Please."

He studied her with bloodshot eyes that had a kind of yearning in them. "Okay. Forget it."

"I can't," she said.

"Ssh, never mind."

Murana could scarcely eat a thing, and when they got home he had just enough time to pack before catching his bus.

This time Murana wept. And she didn't care who saw. She didn't wait until he'd boarded the bus, either.

"Aw, Sissy . . ." When Lyman smiled, his teeth were faintly shadowed with boysenberry syrup.

For just a second, Murana tried to hold him back as he started for the doorway of the panting bus. A few friends, their farewells already said, stepped back respectfully. The coach, Miles Comstock, put on a pair of sunglasses and studied the dappled autumn sky.

"You be a good girl now till I get back, hear?" He gently removed his sister's arms from his neck. "Drink some milk shakes. Fatten yourself up a mite." His eyes were filling with tears.

"I'll pray," Murana whispered, her fingers plucking at the heavy sleeve of his uniform.

Lyman pulled away.

She knew he wouldn't be coming back.

He came back a year and a half later in the spring of 1972. Not all the way back—only as far as the VA Hospital in Lexington. And not all of him—something seemed to be missing.

There was a story in the *Mount Vadalia Sentinel*, LOCAL HERO RETURNS, and they used the picture that had been taken at the end of basic training. Murana wondered how the paper got it. She'd never have given it to them herself. Besides, her brother wasn't home yet. Not really *home*. The story talked about Lyman's "acts of bravery" and his decorations and his football record. Murana was proud, but somehow uneasy, too. She didn't understand the word "hero." Not how they meant it at the paper, anyhow. To her, Lyman Gene had been a hero all along. The thing that mattered was, he was alive. All she knew was that Bubba was a gift from God and a living miracle, and it was up to her to see to him, like always.

The VA Hospital looked just like a college, she thought. There were so many large, serious-looking buildings, cinnamon-colored brick, set in a careful pattern on the bright clipped lawns. Soldiers were guarding the gate, though, and men in bathrobes walked or wheeled along cement pathways. It was a fine spring day. Nurses, white from head to toe, walked briskly between doorways. Still, if you took away the nurses and wheelchairs and got the young men properly dressed, it might have been a college.

When she got her first glimpse of him, Lyman Gene was sitting in a large black-and-white-tiled room down the hall from the room they'd told her was his.

Murana had to hang back in the hallway for a moment to get hold of herself before going in to see him. It had been a terrible shock, running in to room 413 and seeing that empty bed, all neatly made up, not a wrinkle on the pillowcase. She'd thought the worst, of course. As she had all along. She was still quaking.

Downstairs Riley and Glenda McCue were waiting for her

in the main lobby. Surely she'd want to see her brother alone, in private, first, they'd said. It seemed only right. But now Murana wished they were here, on either side of her, to hold her up.

She clung to a portion of the cold metal railings that lined the corridor and tried to catch her breath. He was in there. She could see him.

He was watching television with a group of boys, a look of listening on his face. His lips moved soundlessly.

The doctor warned she'd find him changed, but he looked just the same to her. Well, a little older maybe. From the doorway, Lyman Gene did look older, and perhaps not quite so big as she remembered. But right fit, just the same.

"Physically he is fine," the doctor, Colonel O'Malley, had told her. Murana noticed he looked at the top of her head, rather than into her eyes.

"What's the matter with him?" she whispered. "Nothing?"

"Physically . . . no."

"Then why are you keeping him?"

The colonel had sighed and glanced out the window. A figure in a tan bathrobe hobbled across the lawn below, bright aluminum crutches glittering in the sun.

"You might say your brother has been . . . traumatized."

"An operation?"

"No, no. Nothing like that. He's suffered some manner of shock."

"How?"

The doctor shrugged.

"He's all I have," Murana said. "You'd best be plain."

For the first time, the colonel looked directly at her. His stern features softened with sympathy, and his voice sounded tired. "Your brother has had something like an injury to his mind, Miss Bill. You are apt to find him, as I said, changed."

"Changed *how*?" She leaned forward and placed her hands on the edge of the doctor's desk. They were balled into fists.

He took off his steel-framed glasses and stared intently at her forehead. "I'm afraid he doesn't talk."

For a second, Murana was terrified. She imagined her brother stone-cold and silent as a statue. But then, unaccountably, she found herself picturing the three little brass figures of monkeys on Pa's desk—the third one had his paws pressed over his mouth. But underneath, he was smiling. You could tell because of the way his eyes were all squinched up.

She felt a tremendous rush of relief. Her hands loosened and dropped back down to her lap.

"He'll talk to me," she said.

The colonel smiled as he rose to show her courteously to the door. "I wish you luck, of course," he said, "but—"

Murana, pretending to smooth her hair, pressed her hands over her ears.

There he was, the same as ever, staring at the television, giving the eye to some pretty blond actress. Murana recognized her: a shapely girl who was supposed to be a genie out of a bottle. She wore a flimsy costume showing her belly button and got into all sorts of trouble because of doing magic mischief and getting caught at it by this man in a uniform who was too foolish to see how he was really in love with her.

Lyman cocked his head to one side.

On the television there was a puff of smoke and the blonde disappeared. The television audience laughed. Some of the boys in the VA Hospital did, too. Lyman's face was turned away from the door, so Murana couldn't see his expression, but she knew he must be smiling.

As she entered the black-and-white-tiled room, a commercial came on. Most of the boys kept right on watching. Lyman Gene stared down at his knees, where his hands were sprawled, still and lifeless-looking.

Murana took great care not to startle him. With the heels

of her navy blue pumps clicking on the black-and-white squares, she cut a wide circle around his chair to approach him from the front.

"Bubba?"

He looked up. She saw the slight movement of his mouth, nothing so definite as words. His gray eyes were patient and noncommittal, reserving judgment.

Murana kept moving toward him, slowly, one measured step at a time. Her hands were reaching for him. "It's me," she said.

His lips flickered. Then he was staring past her again to the television commercial, a linoleum floor with stars dancing on it, winding in a ring around a woman with a mop.

"Bubba...guess I shouldn't call you that anymore. Kinda babyish, I reckon." She touched his cheeks, lightly. His skin was warm to her cold fingers. She leaned down and awkwardly gathered as much of him as could fit in her arms. "Lyman Gene?"

He didn't push her away, but his vast shoulders stiffened as if the embrace pained him. Murana drew back and straightened up. "I prayed," she whispered, feasting her eyes on the sight of him. "Like I promised."

Lyman Gene's gaze remained on the television. His lips parted, showing the tip of his tongue.

"We'll get you back home in no time. Safe and sound."

The genie and the officer came back on the screen. She recited some magical formula with words like "abracadabra" and "hocus-pocus." Suddenly a lion appeared in their living room. The officer yelled and jumped up on a blue velvet sofa and his hat fell off. The lion ate it in one bite.

The audience laughed.

The boys in the black-and-white-tiled room laughed.

Lyman Gene licked his lips, almost smiled.

Murana pressed her fingertips to her eyelids, noticing how red veins of light snaked through the darkness.

Seven months later, Lyman Gene came home to Mount Vadalia.

The town wanted to give him a hero's welcome, a parade and all, but his sister said no. "He's suffered a shock," she said. "He's not ... himself just yet."

"I'm afraid we've done all we can for him," the doctor told her. "Nothing seems to help."

"Getting home will help," Murana said.

"He might be better off here. He needs a great deal of attention."

"I'll see to him."

"There's something else." The colonel polished the lenses of his glasses with the hem of his white coat. "His heart ... a weakness ..."

"You said—" Murana felt herself sinking. "You told me before that nothing happened to him. Physical, I mean."

"That's true. But there is a weakness in his heart."

"A wound?" she whispered.

"Of course not, no. This is surely something the boy had before, from rheumatic fever perhaps. We simply discovered it here. By accident."

"A weakness," Murana said.

"That's right."

"A weakness, a shock—what better reason for a boy to be home?" Murana regarded the doctor sternly.

The VA had no answer for that. In the end, they handed her brother over to her, and Murana swore they'd never get hold of him again.

It was the day before Thanksgiving when he returned. Miles Comstock, the football coach, and his oldest boy Verlie, who meant to be a doctor, drove down to Lexington to pick him up. Murana stayed behind to get everything ready at the house. She moved her brother's belongings from the Ruckus Room back upstairs to his old bedroom. She wanted him right across the hall, in case he needed her in the middle of the night. And she meant for him to wake to sunlight in the mornings. By now, all grown, he'd probably forgotten how he used to like to sleep in the basement anyhow.

Murana restocked the soda fountain, though. Made sure there was plenty of ice cream in the freezer. Tried out the milk-shake machine to see that it still worked. She bought a quart jug of maraschino cherries, bright red, and threw out the old ones that had turned a rusty color.

Lyman Gene was about to turn twenty-one when he came home to stay—a man by the laws of the land and nature. Murana was almost twenty-four. As soon as he returned, though, she realized it was as if she'd got herself a baby.

He did not, for one thing, dress himself. The first morning he was home, Thanksgiving, Murana thought the trip from the hospital had simply worn him out. The second day she asked if he was feeling poorly. On the third morning she took his temperature. It was normal.

"It's because of the hospital, ain't it?" she said.

Lyman Gene sat straight and still in the ladder-back chair beside his bedroom window and stared at the foot of his bed.

"No wonder a body doesn't recover in a place like that, no clothes and all. I'm gonna burn that dun-colored robe, I declare. We'll get you a plaid one, nice and soft, red maybe."

Murana rifled the bird's-eye maple chiffonier and found a pair of chinos, a flannel shirt, and some gray boxer shorts with little sea horses on them.

"Now, where's all your socks? I couldn't find a one in this house. And what are we gonna do for shoes?"

Lyman Gene studied the pattern of the Cathedral Window quilt on his bed.

"You wait right here," his sister said.

In a moment, she was back, carrying his old black high-tops, stored in her own closet since the week their parents had died. "Think you can still squeeze into these?" She banged the two gigantic sneakers together to shake the dust from them. "Just for now . . . long enough to get you over to Mr. Willis and buy some new ones. And I don't want to hear no arguments, either. I ain't having these floors marked up with no army boots, so don't get you any notions about that."

Murana stacked the clothes, the shoes on top, and set them on her brother's lap. "Now I'll be back in two shakes, and I want to find you dressed, hear?"

When she returned ten minutes later, Lyman Gene was sitting in the ladder-back chair beside the window. The pile of folded clothes was on the floor at his feet, the shoes still on top.

Murana sighed. "Well, I reckon we'll let it go for now."

She crossed the hall to her own bedroom and stood looking into the dresser mirror for several minutes. Her long, homely face was bewildered, her eyes full of grief.

On the marble top of the dresser, an old black-and-white photograph showed Clive and Mary Alice standing together in front of the house. Lyman Gene, in a stroller, was between them. Murana, off to one side, was looking away from the camera.

The past squeezed up against her, a suffocating thing. She recalled how, even then, hardly more than a baby herself, she'd wanted Lyman Gene all for her own. Bubba. How she'd begged to bathe and change and feed him, sat watching over his crib for hours.

Now it was up to her, alone, to see to him.

She went back into his room. "We *won't* let it go," she said. "Nossir."

She grasped his arms and tried to raise him from the chair. He was a dead weight.

"Git up."

Lyman Gene looked at her, his eyes perfectly calm, and rose from the chair.

Still exerting force, Murana staggered back and caught herself on the edge of the closet door.

"Well, that's better."

With unsteady hands, she began to undo the knot in his bathrobe sash.

The first few days, dressing and undressing him seemed an awful ordeal. Murana hadn't seen her brother fully unclothed since he'd stopped wearing diapers. In fact, she'd never seen any man naked. But after all, she told herself, Bubba was a baby again, at least for the time being. And if he had to learn from scratch how to dress himself, who else was going to teach him?

He stood before her without shame, his face blank, and looked right at her. Murana thought she couldn't bear it—his lack of shame. She talked a mile a minute, her face red and miserable, and eventually learned to help him into his underwear while standing in back of him. The sight of his smooth white behind made it easier to pretend that she was caring for a child.

When she bathed him, however, there was nothing she could avoid. It took two weeks before she was able to perform this intimate task without trembling for hours afterward. "Thy brother's nakedness"—a phrase from the Bible, she thought. She tried to look it up but couldn't find it. She considered asking the priest when she went to Confession, but what could a priest tell her that she didn't already know? If a body was unclean, you bathed it. If your brother was naked, you put clothes on him. It was that simple. But it wasn't easy.

Some things were easy, though. Feeding him, for one thing. Whatever the shock her brother had suffered in war, it seemed to have given him a powerful appetite. Lyman Gene had always been a good eater, with a particular fondness for his sister's cooking. Even while their parents were alive, he'd teased and bribed to get her to make things for him. He swore no one—not Mama, not even Miss Belle Kinney the home ec teacher—made piecrust and rolls like Murana's. When he was only a small boy, he pronounced hers the best grilled cheese, the creamiest cocoa, the chewiest brownies. It got to be a family joke, how he'd scheme to lure her into the kitchen and put her to work.

Murana didn't mind a bit. Watching her brother wolf down something she'd made had always been her greatest pleasure. But she'd scarcely cooked the whole time he was gone. Her own appetite was meager and plain, and with Lyman Gene away from home, Murana had lost her taste for just about everything. The second summer she'd even let the gardening and canning go. There were still mason jars of corn relish, bread-and-butter pickles, spiced peaches and pickled beets and chowchow left from earlier seasons. And nobody to feed them to.

Once Lyman was settled, Murana passed her days in the kitchen again. She baked cakes and pies and bread. She roasted chickens and legs of lamb and briskets of beef. She chopped vegetables and nutmeats, beat egg whites with sugar until they became frothy clouds, then glistening mountains.

At first she feared she might have forgotten it all: how to skim the fat from soup, how to knead dough just long enough, how to get the lumps out of gravy but leave a few in mashed potatoes. The old rhythms and secrets came back, though, and seeing Lyman Gene with his mouth full and his plate empty gave her confidence.

He wouldn't come down to the dining room. He wouldn't even eat at the kitchen table. While he was quite agreeable about most everything else, standing subdued so she could dress him, stepping cooperatively into the tub, when it came time for meals Lyman Gene refused to budge from his room. Murana decided this, too, was a habit carried over from hospital ways. It would pass in time. Until then, carrying trays to him wasn't any trouble; she saw no reason to make an issue of it.

Like the mother of a newborn infant, she learned to sleep lightly, her ear always awaiting sound of him. She left a night-light burning in the hall, another at his bedside. Her slippers lay where she could step right into them.

Because she was attuned, even in sleep, to his every movement, she knew he traveled the house at night. His favorite place was the kitchen pantry. He'd eat anything that was left from supper. Sometimes even things Murana had made for the next day.

The second week he was home, on Saturday night, Lyman Gene ate the sour-cream raisin pie Murana had baked for Sunday dinner. All of it. She scolded him and missed her ride to church with the McCues because she had to make another dessert.

When she'd caught him in the pantry at midnight, her brother had looked up and, for the first time in more than two years, truly smiled at her. It wasn't a broad smile. He didn't show his teeth. Still, it seemed like a gift to Murana, and she was sure he offered it in apology.

The next night, though, she heard him downstairs again. Running to see what he was up to, she found him holding the empty cellophane wrapper from a dozen jelly doughnuts she'd bought for breakfast. He was standing by the sink. When he grinned at her, there was a ring of powdered sugar around his mouth. And a bright streak of currant jelly on his lower lip.

No matter how much she bought, and no matter how much she cooked, there never seemed to be enough to satisfy him. She learned to hide food outside the kitchen, not to cook ahead of time. She kept things frozen until the last minute, hid the can opener, and got accustomed to this way of managing.

. . .

Lyman Gene's silence was the hardest thing. Murana was sure it wouldn't last, but her brother's speechlessness terrified her. From the time they were children, he'd been the talkative one. He chattered a mile a minute, telling stories and lies, boasting, teasing ... and yes, comforting her. To have the sound of his voice denied her made Murana's existence seem precarious.

The VA doctors had offered little encouragement.

"When is he likely to get it back?" she asked.

"It's impossible to say," Colonel O'Malley had told her, "since we don't really know why he lost it in the first place."

It: she kept remembering an expression her mother had used whenever shyness overcame Murana in front of company: "Cat got your tongue?" That cat had never seemed real, not the way the Angel of Mischief did. But now she began to think of the critter as her flesh-and-blood enemy. She'd catch that cat and skin it alive. Nine times, if need be.

"He'll talk," she said.

The colonel had shrugged. "I hope so." There was anything but hope in his tone.

He would. Murana was sure of it. Lyman would talk to her. And in the meantime, she'd speak for the both of them.

When Lyman Gene first came home, Murana spoke to him in a gentle murmur, hardly above a whisper, and mostly in the future tense. "It'll be all right, Bubba. You'll see. We're gonna get you well and strong and nothing will ever hurt you again. Everything'll be fine." She repeated the same vague reassurances over and over again. And the more worried she herself became as she got acquainted with the depths of her brother's helplessness, the more ardently she promised there was nothing to worry about. "I'm gonna take such good care of you, just see if I don't ... you'll be back to your old self in no time."

As things settled down into routine and Murana accustomed

herself to Lyman Gene's silence, her conversation broadened. She told him what was in the morning paper. She recounted neighbors' visits word for word. Chance meetings in the store, Sunday sermons, early-morning radio shows were reenacted. Bland as they were, she served her days to him on a platter, generous and garnished. It gave a heightened color and shapeliness to her life, this need to relay its detail to her brother who kept to his room as if imprisoned. And Murana was sure what she was doing was paving the road to his recovery. She would maintain his connection to the world so that when he was ready, he'd have no trouble finding his way back. She asked the coach's wife to lend her old copies of the high-school paper, *The Cardinal,* so she could read to Lyman Gene about the football seasons he'd missed.

Her greatest source of conversation, however, was Lyman Gene himself. Had she had to rely solely upon the goings-on in the household and the town, she'd soon have run out of subjects. But in worrying over that, she'd overlooked the most important thing: she wasn't talking just for herself. Now she was entitled, indeed duty-bound, to speak for her brother.

Being Lyman Gene's mouthpiece opened up a whole new world. Barriers to the past went down. The present became round and faceted and glittering, like a diamond. And the future widened and widened until it seemed to hold all sorts of possibilities so astonishing that Murana herself could never have imagined them. She felt like a different person. Serving as her brother's tongue seemed to endow her with his eyes and ears, and his heart as well. Merely herself, she often felt lost, afraid of her own shadow. Inhabiting him, however, lent her new capacities. She became bold and inventive. Her courage grew. His was a life worth fighting for.

All of her love was set in motion. She was free to adore her brother, and to assume his love for her. And as she spoke for him, she began to feel for him so deeply that she no longer knew where she herself ended and he began.

She didn't care. The distinction was hardly worth making.

And sometimes, as she watched him sitting in silence and gazing out the window toward the mountains, she would see his lips move...

Yes, his lips would move a little, as his eyes roamed over the foothills. He'd come back, Murana thought, all of him.

She just knew it.

*M*r. and Mrs. Riley McCue sat in their family room, a recently completed addition to their colonial raised ranch in the Thoroughbred Estates. It was mid-August, an oppressively hot night, but the house at the end of the cul-de-sac on Man o' War Lane had central air-conditioning. The room, cool and new, smelled like the inside of a car fresh off the assembly line.

Glenda McCue kicked off one yellow satin mule and burrowed her toes into the persimmon shag carpeting.

Her husband smiled. "Right out of a magazine. You sure do have the knack of decorating, honey." He leaned back and took a gulp from a tall frosted glass with red golf tees painted on it. "Woo-eee, this daiquiri mix is fearsome bad!"

"It ain't right, Rile."

He made a pointed effort to misconstrue her familiar conversational gambit. He'd had enough problems for one day. "Right? It's downright awful."

"I wasn't talkin' about your damn-fool drink and you know it."

"And I'd be a jackass in ballet slippers if I was to try side-steppin' what you mean to tell me, huh?"

"Never mind the country-boy routine. I know you from Cincinnati, remember?"

Riley grinned. "Down-home do sell them see-dans, though."

"I ain't in the market."

"What's the trouble?"

"Them Bill children . . . it just ain't right."

"Way L.T. over to the Savings and Loan tells it, they ain't got a worry in the world."

"Money's not what I mean."

Riley sighed. "Yeah, I know. Don't know what we can *do* about it, is the problem."

"I was over there this afternoon . . . just stopped by to say hello and see how they're getting on. It's really pitiful, you know."

"He ain't any better?"

"He ain't hardly *human*. But it's her worries me."

"Listen, honey, it'd wear anybody down."

"But that's just it—she acts like it's nothin' at all. It'd be healthier, her showing a few signs of wear and tear. She's happy as a cat in a creamery."

"Now who's doin' the hayseed number?"

Glenda smiled fondly at her husband and tucked her legs, tanned from long afternoons around the golf club pool, under the loose folds of her tricot nightgown. Her satisfied glance took in the entire room. "Looks like we're here to stay. Might as well join 'em."

"Body could do worse," Riley said.

"He ought to be back to that VA."

"Try telling that to his big sister."

"Not me, sweetheart."

"So what's the point?"

"So *somebody* should, is the point. Tell her. It's no kinda life for a girl."

"She's not exactly a girl."

"She is, Rile. Not that a soul'd know it. With him on her hands, she's got to lookin' like some old biddy. You know how old she is?"

Riley sighed, closing his eyes. The unwanted vision followed him inward: the mangled remains of Clive and Mary Alice Bill. Riley McCue was the one they called when the bodies had to be identified. "To spare the kids," the state trooper said. Riley'd done that part all right. The corpses hadn't seemed real. But when he saw what was left of that week-old Belvedere, he'd thrown up in a ditch at the side of the road. The force it would take to do that to a car...that was something he could imagine.

"You lose track of time," he said.

"She's twenty-four, Rile. Twenty-four."

"You want me to talk to her."

"Somebody ought to. It ain't healthy."

"Ain't hardly our business," Riley said.

"Tell you the truth, I never did know quite what to make of them, Clive and Mary Alice. Kinda standoffish in their way, I guess."

"Hard folks to know," Riley agreed.

"Seemed to me it was mostly bein' wrapped up in each other, though. Each other and them two kids."

"Wrapped up is right. And off in the clouds somewheres."

"Okay. But they called us friends, Rile. And if we wasn't, who was?"

Glenda walked over to the picture window and stood peering out into the dark yard. Her thin, angular body—so obstinate, refusing to yield the children they'd both wanted—showed through the sheer fabric of her nightgown. Riley McCue recalled how soft she'd looked when he married her nearly twenty years ago. She'd been twenty-four then herself.

"You lose track of time," he repeated. "You surely do."

She didn't turn around. "How long since you seen him?"

"Quite a spell, I guess."

"He must weigh three hundred pounds. Maybe more."

"What—"

"She's killing the both of them...'cause she don't know

what else to do. While we just sit here."

"I'll do something," Riley promised. "Don't know what, but something."

The following week, Riley McCue paid Murana a call.

He had to admit the girl's appearance was startling. She might have been forty—and had a hard life. There was scarcely a trace of color to her complexion, nor gloss to her hair. Her large frame was skeletal. She looked bone-dry, used up.

She sat on the front steps of the peeling yellow house. The skirt of her gray seersucker dress was hiked up to form a hammock between her bony knees. In spite of the heat, she wore stockings, cheap dime-store hose with a harsh orange cast. Her lap was piled high with pole beans, from which she was deftly snapping the ends before dropping them into a blue speckled canning pot.

When Riley McCue's gleaming white Imperial pulled into the drive, Murana looked up expectantly. As soon as she recognized her visitor, a smile of pleasure stretched her drawn face tight across her enormous teeth. He recalled her as a child, homely as sin and good as gold. Spitting image of her daddy that way . . .

"Why, Mr. McCue . . . how nice!"

She hastily pulled her skirt down, scattering a few beans on the steps.

Riley grinned. "Stay right where you are, Murana. I ain't got all afternoon to help you pick up them beans." He stooped and gathered the few that had fallen, whistling as he inspected them. "Whoppers," he said. "Yours?"

"From right out back here. You'll take some home to Miz McCue?"

"Don't mind if I do. These are beauties."

Murana stood up awkwardly and, holding the front of her skirt, backed up the steps. She slid the beans onto the seat of the porch glider.

"Come in where it's cool. I made us some pink lemonade just now."

"Pink?"

"Bubba likes it best thataway."

"Well, so do I." He followed her through the door.

The house, he saw, was neat as a pin, and fresh. Only the girl herself looked the worse for wear.

"Where's young Lyman?"

"Havin' him a nap . . . he needs a good bit of rest."

"Sure thing. I was hoping I might see him, though . . ."

"He's coming along right nicely." McCue saw that the subject was meant to be closed.

"Glad to hear it," he muttered.

They sat in the cool, dim parlor on two platform rockers half-facing each other in front of the fireplace. Along with the lemonade, Murana brought in several plates of cookies. At first he declined them, saying it was nearly suppertime. But Murana looked so distressed that he began to eat anyway, claiming he couldn't resist.

"Just took a marble cake from the oven . . . still warm."

"Aw, I couldn't," he said.

"You'll carry some home, then."

He didn't try to argue with her.

"Glenda tells me . . ." he began uneasily.

Murana looked alarmed. "Yes, she come by to see us the other day. Sweetest woman ever lived, that wife of yours. And she—"

"Murana?"

"Mr. McCue?" She looked down at her large hands, tightly clasped together in her lap.

"I'd say it's high time you started calling us by our given names, for one thing."

"All right."

"And I'd like to ask your permission to talk to you like a . . . like a Dutch uncle."

"Pardon?"

"Like kin," he said.

Her face paled.

"We worry about you, Glenda and me."

"I don't understand."

Riley inhaled slowly, setting down his glass. "I think you do, girl. I think you understand right well that you're in way over your head here."

"Why, we're managing fine. Just fine. Have I done something wrong?"

Too late, he saw that he'd put her in a panic. "Wrong? Of course not. It's just that it's too much."

She looked away. On the mantel, a cuckoo clock emitted a little grinding sound, then began to chirp and chime. Suddenly, Murana smiled. "Lyman Gene loved that clock so when he was a boy. I might should carry it up to his room . . . why didn't I think of it before?"

"Murana . . ."

"I know you mean it kindly, Mr. . . . Riley. But doing for him's pure joy for me."

"He belongs back to the VA, honey."

"He belongs," Murana said, "to me."

Before he knew what hit him, Riley McCue was back in his white Imperial, heading into the sunset toward the Thoroughbred Estates.

A sack of pole beans and a chunk of marble cake on a foil plate were on the seat beside him. They wouldn't do the trick, he knew . . .

What in this dog-eared world was he going to tell his wife?

"My, them plum dumplings was a delight . . . if I do say so myself. Don't know what the Lord was thinkin' of when He made the peach and plum season so short. Why, winter wouldn't be half so bad if a body could have him a decent piece of fruit now and then, something a step up from a apple or orange. I surely ain't one for takin' issue with the Bible, but it seems mighty suspicious to me, Adam and Eve gettin' in such a big to-do over a ordinary apple. You ask me, musta been a peach they took. Or one of them fancy expensive things ... whatchacallit, avocado. The God of this whole world wouldn't put up such an almighty fuss over one common apple, would He?

"Land, I near forgot to tell you! Mr. Riley McCue come by to pay us a call this afternoon. Such a kindly man, how he always takes interest in the other person and all. He was askin' for you, of course. But it was right in the middle of the 'Dialin' for Dollars' movie, so I said you was takin' a nap. What was it today? Oh, yes, that one where Jerry Lewis is a bellhop in a big hotel and gets into all that tomfoolery. I seen that one before myself. 'Well, I'll tell my brother you was askin' for him, Mr. Riley McCue,' I say. 'Lyman Gene'll be right pleased. Yes, he's fit as a fiddle, thank you kindly.'

"You should have seen the way he took to them cookies I made this morning. The ones with the jam in particular. And he was downright jealous of our pole beans. I give him some to take home.

"But I never got around to telling you what he come by for, did I? It was the sweetest thing. 'Murana,' he says, 'me an' Miz McCue think of you and your brother just like kin. We want you to know that. And if there's ever a thing in this world you need, why you only say so, hear?'

"'We'll surely do that, Mr. Riley McCue,' I said. 'And my brother and me are right grateful. Only don't you folks worry yourself none on our account. Long as they got each other, Lyman Gene and Murana Bill is taken care of. Yessir. Don't you give that a second thought.'"

Lyman Gene scanned the clouds of steam in the mirror above the bathroom sink, as he parted his knees to let his sister run a washcloth between them.

.　　.　　.

The year that Lyman Gene came back home, the town of Mount Vadalia finally got its very own Catholic church. It still wouldn't have a priest. Not yet, anyway. But visiting priests would come from around the diocese to offer Mass each Sunday.

For Murana this was a sign: she saw the hand of God reaching directly down from Heaven and ministering to her every need. A convergence of blessings, her brother and her Lord both right here in town. But the greatest wonder was that the church was to be in the same building where her father had labored and prospered. The very notion filled Murana with awe—it seemed like God was looking after her personally.

The diocese bought the old storefront on Main Street for a song, refurbished it with a lick and a prayer. The shelves and bins came down easily enough, and Riley McCue sent a work crew over to sand and whitewash the walls. Covered with marbelized contact paper, the long counter at the rear of the store did fine for an altar. Thirty-five folding chairs were donated by Monsignor Shea at St. Boniface. Then the Catholic ladies of Mount Vadalia took over:

Mr. L. T. Moody's wife, Celia, and her sister Claudelle, who came from Florida to spend the summer, stitched and embroidered all the altar cloths by hand. They persuaded Mr. Willis, the Baptist proprietor of the dry goods store, to get the vestment fabrics at cost, and arranged for the sewing to be done by the Carmelite Sisters in Lexington.

In a fine neighborly gesture, the Women's Club of Calvary Hill Third Baptist made a cash donation to cover the cost of hymnals. The Men's Club gave two long-handled offering baskets.

Glenda McCue donated her late mother's parlor organ and the little petit-point swivel stool that went with it. She also came up with two etched-glass light fixtures for the ceiling and a pair of silverplate candelabra to adorn the altar.

But the glory of glories was the doing of Miss Peggy Anne Sligo, the art teacher for the county schools. Working with the light touch of an angel and the fiery vision of a prophet, Peggy Anne laid a design of colored cellophane on the big plate-glass windows. When she'd finished with them, they looked for all the world like real stained glass. A Holy Ghost in a sunburst . . . lilies . . . a starry crown. And in the very center, the Sacred Heart, entwined in thorny bramble, drops of blood the color of garnets dripping from it.

Murana couldn't bear to look for long. Overwhelmed, she turned and embraced Peggy Anne. "What wonders thou hast wrought!" she whispered.

Blushing, fiercely pleased, Peggy Anne knelt and began to gather up the bright, transparent scraps from the sawdust-coated floor. "It's a simple enough kind of praise," she said.

"It's a mighty creation," Murana told her. "A joyful noise to the eye."

"Wish I'd of had the Last Supper in me," Peggy Anne said.

A parish council was formed, with Riley McCue as president, L. T. Moody as treasurer. Murana's name was proposed for corresponding secretary, but she declined. Her handwriting was an abomination, she said. She volunteered to see to flowers, refreshments, and such.

From the moment she heard the wonderful news of the new church, Murana discussed the matter passionately and perpetually with her brother. She longed to have a hand in making the Lord's house comfortable, especially since it was going to be on the very spot where her earthly father had passed his days. If only she were artistic like Peggy Anne, or good with her hands like Mrs. L. T. Moody, or rich like the Riley McCues . . .

Then she felt ashamed. Surely the good Lord didn't mean His coming to town to fill her heart with envy and ingratitude. She reminded herself what He said about the lilies of the field and the birds of the air and rich men passing through the eye of a needle. Still, she intended to find some way of doing her part.

"Maybe I shoulda said yes to being secretary, you think?

Writing all them letters would have been penance, at least. But I don't believe the Lord cares for penance half so much as charity. And there'd be no mercy in it, disgracing Him with those cramped, cockeyed letters of mine.

"I'd thought to make draperies for the windows, red velvet maybe, with braidlike cords... you know how they do? But then Peggy Anne got hold of that colored plastic wrap... well, it's like a miracle what she did. You should see when the sun shines through, like looking a whole band of angels in the eye. No drapes could do like that.

"God's been good to us, Bubba. We got more than most folks. You know how Banker Moody's always sayin' we got nothin' to worry about? Well, I been thinking maybe we could do with a bit less, you know? We ought to give something... for Mama and Pa, as well as us. Why, just imagine how proud they'd be, knowing where the church is. It's part of our family, in a way... almost like our home and the Lord's come visitin' and picked us to stay with. It's a honor, and that's a fact."

Later, it would seem to Murana that she and Lyman Gene had worked the problem out together. In fact, she told the Riley McCues it was her brother's own idea:

She cashed in some savings bonds, five hundred dollars, and bought a bronze holy water font. She ordered it all the way from New York City—Della Croce Religious Articles, Ltd. The heavy greenish bowl was scalloped like a seashell, supported by cherubs at either side, with a flower garland circling the rim. On the part that fastened flush to the wall, there was a small brass plaque: "In loving memory of Mr. and Mrs. Clive Bill from their children Lyman Gene and Murana."

Every Sunday for years afterward, as she dipped her rough fingers into the cool, slightly oily-feeling water to bless herself, Murana seemed to catch the scents of her mother's cologne, her father's shaving soap. Touching her own forehead, she recalled how her parents' faces would shine after they'd taken Communion, how their voices would blend and soar with the hymns that turned to mush in other folks' mouths. And time after time, Murana remembered, Mama had told her she needn't have a worry in the world. "Long as you got your Church and your family, you have everything you need to get you through this life."

The new church was dedicated on the first Sunday of May, and the bishop came all the way from Louisville to officiate. A frail elderly man without hair, he looked hot and burdened by his heavy vestments and miter.

Although there were only a handful of Catholics in Mount Vadalia, there weren't nearly enough chairs for all who attended the special Mass and dedication ceremony. Town officials, pastors of neighboring churches, and a good many of the merely curious came.

The sky was thick and threatening; a storm was near. Murana was disappointed, for she'd imagined this grand occasion many times, Lyman Gene sitting beside her and the sun throwing brilliant swaths of light through Peggy Anne's glorious windows. The bishop, she thought, would look like Gregory Peck. Or Senator John Sherman Cooper. She bowed her head for the Confiteor and worried that her brother, home alone, might have found the corn pudding she made for supper.

At the Consecration, however, she lifted her eyes to the host. Held tenderly toward the raftered ceiling of her father's store by the bishop's holy hands, the wafer seemed to shine with a pure white glow that could only be grace. "For this is My Body..." Murana buried her face in her hands and, with tears seeping through her fingers, she thanked Him: for her brother and her faith, for her life.

"I shall not want," she prayed.

"Happy are those who are called to His supper," the bishop said.

.   .   .

"Meanin' no disrespect," Murana said, "but I never guessed he'd be so well on. And puny, too. A little sliver of a man, all bogged down with them fancy robes...that huge ring on that mite of a hand..."

Lyman Gene looked past her, the tip of a chicken wing poking out from the corner of his mouth.

"Save room for dessert, now," she said. "I s'pose a bishop's only a man like everybody else, but I somehow expected he'd *look* different, you know?"

Her brother reached for the sweet potatoes, upending the serving dish over his plate.

"Might as well polish them off. They're never the same reheated."

Downstairs in the kitchen the oven timer went off with a rude buzz.

"Lord a mighty, I forgot about them rolls!"

As his sister dashed from the room, Lyman Gene snatched her dinner—small portions, scarcely touched—and emptied her plate onto his own. Then, hunching his shoulders over the card table, his forearms forming a protective circle around the food, he resumed eating. The tendons in his jaw and throat worked urgently.

5

*I*t wasn't right. Maybe she knew all along, and just wouldn't let herself see. But Doc Purchase told her in no uncertain terms.

"At this rate, he's going to *die*," he said.

Old Arthur Purchase wasn't one of those cold-eyed, knife-lipped doctors like at the VA. He'd been a friend of Pa's. His face was round and rosy and smooth, like he'd been a stranger to worry his whole life long. But he was worried now, and telling her so.

Murana stared back at him, distressed. Her graying brown hair, tight with a new home permanent wave, felt damp and prickly on the back of her neck. It still had a faint skunky odor.

"It's that heart of his, girl. Can't bear the weight."

Murana sat quiet for another moment. Her strong, reddened hands were splayed along the edge of the table in mute helplessness. Her gaze dropped from the doctor's troubled face to the smoky topaz in her father's high-school class ring, worn on the middle finger of her right hand. Gray knitting wool wound around its back kept it from slipping off her finger.

"He's all I've got."

"So he is," Doc Purchase said.

She went to the range and picked up the percolator. She

paused there, studying the distorted upper half of her face in the dented aluminum. Her eyes looked two different sizes.

Behind her, the doctor's voice was reasonable. "All the more reason, ain't it?"

Murana refilled his cup. Then, without thinking to ask if he wanted it, she cut him another wedge of lemon-filled coconut cake. Her hand was trembling as she lowered it to his plate. She felt his waiting, his wanting something of her.

"It's hard to deny him," she said.

"You're just not used to it, is all."

She sighed. "That's God's truth."

"Which don't make it sacred."

Murana got up from the table again, wringing her hands in front of her chest. She took a long, deep breath. Then she dusted her hands together, lightly, three times.

It was the gesture of a woman who meant to move domestic mountains, take grown men in tow, and there was a familiarity about it. Maybe he was imagining things, Arthur Purchase thought, but for one startling instant, the girl did seem to resemble her mother powerfully.

"You'd best heed me, now," he said.

Murana nodded. Then she smiled at him, sweet as pie, and Doc Purchase knew the maternal likeness existed in more than just his mind. Mary Alice Bill, still lying in childbed after the birth of the boy, had given him just such a look when he advised her against more babies. Another delivery like that one would have killed her for certain, and Doc had minced no words in telling her so.

Smiling agreeably, she'd given him back some damn-fool nonsense about the Church and how if God meant her to have more children, He'd see to it she did, with no harm. Just as she'd die if her time was at hand. She was willing to take her chances. Only "God's will" was what she called it. The doctor called it Russian roulette. Well, that's what it *was*. But by luck or by blessing, she'd won. There were no more pregnancies.

Miss Murana could smile all she liked, Arthur Purchase thought. Agree with him until they were both blue in the face. She still couldn't hide it from him—she had a mind of her own, a regular stubborn streak like her mama. And there was going to be a whole lot more trouble visiting this house if the girl figured *God* was likely to oversee her brother's eating habits or patch up that leaky heart of his without a little cooperation from her.

Doc Purchase gave Murana a severe look. "Doctor's orders," he said.

She nodded obediently, and smiled.

Murana tried. She tried everything she could think of. She arranged platters of raw vegetables, Jell-O, fruit, and cottage cheese, vivid and intricate as Mexican mosaics. She made her own melba toast and sugarless preserves, huge caldrons of broths and teas. She cooked chickens, searing her fingers to tear off the skin and dispose of it before the fragrance of roasting fat lured her brother down the stairs.

White meat, grapefruit compote, radish roses: Lyman Gene devoured everything she offered, foraged for what she withheld, silently begged for more. Dismantled by his accusing stares, she prepared in modest batches the dishes that he favored. Finding no more in the kitchen, he sobbed with rage and, once, hurled one of Mama's best bone china plates at her. She ducked. It shattered. They both wept, Murana more repentantly than her brother.

One night she awoke and heard him in the kitchen. Clutching her bathrobe together, the sash dragging behind her, she crept down the stairway. Through the kitchen entryway she saw him clearing the pantry shelves. He'd found the can opener, hidden in the piano bench.

When he saw her watching him, Lyman Gene shifted his great bulk to block her from the counter, where rows of tins were lined up, their sharp flaps already raised.

The only light in the room fell from the yawning door of the Frigidaire, emptied now of milk, juice, staples, condiments, everything. Lyman Gene's face looked pale and bloated in the eerie illumination. When his mouth twisted in a terrible sweet smile, Murana understood that he would fight her, perhaps even kill her, for the block of cheddar cheese concealed in the pie safe, for the roll of Life Savers upstairs in her purse.

She turned and went back up to bed.

When she came down in the morning, she found an elaborate pyramid of tin cans in the center of the kitchen table. He'd removed the lids and labels and washed the insides so that she couldn't even calculate what he'd devoured.

When the low-calorie menus, cajolery, and deception all failed, Murana tried sterner measures, tactics born of desperation.

The worst thing—and she'd done it only once—was locking Lyman Gene in his room.

For an entire day and night, he'd sobbed without stopping, filling the house with wordless bellows of fury and desolation.

Murana sat in the parlor, her hands pressed to her ears. Tears streaked her face. She tried to eat supper—just some soup and crackers—but she was throwing it up in the toilet bowl before she'd taken more than a few bites. She sat up the whole night, knowing any attempt at sleep would be useless. For the first time in weeks, she picked up Mama's Hosanna Quilt, but her hands seemed to have lost their feel for the work. Her stitches were crude and crooked again. She knew she'd have to rip them out.

It was five o'clock in the morning before he started quieting. He made some exhausted whimpering sounds for a while, sounds that pierced his sister's heart more painfully than his louder wails. Then, at last, the wracked house grew still.

In one of the platform rockers near the fireplace, Murana pushed her feet against the faded hooked rug. The chair glided back and forth in little mincing steps that reminded her of the way brides walked up the aisle: right-slip-stop, left-slip-stop...

Slowly, her head dropped back to rest on the high carved edge of the chair back. She reached into her deep apron pocket and pulled out a string of blue crystal rosary beads. They glittered in a pool of lamplight on her lap as her fingers groped automatically, bead to bead, through the Sorrowful Mysteries.

"Glory be to the Father and to the Son..."

The Glory Bee.

She hadn't thought of it in years. Bubba had been like a puppy then, only four or five years old, all squirms and teeth and feet too big for him. Too young for church, really, but Mama and Pa took him along anyway, just like they'd taken Murana almost from the day she was born. Only their little girl, even as an infant, had known to keep still. Pa, teasing her surely, used to tell how the first word out of her baby mouth was "Amen"—and just at the right place, too.

The boy, however, was a holy terror at church—no different than at home. Except a mite worse, maybe, he did hate confinement so. He'd climb joyously over the pews, an obstacle course meant just for him. Shouted nursery rhymes and radio slogans and orders throughout the sermon, as if heckling the priest. Why once, right at the very Consecration. Hearing the chimes as the host was elevated, he'd yelled "Sound off for Chesterfield!" and gone staggering toward the altar like an unruly drunk until Pa'd caught him up and hustled him, shrieking, out to the vestibule.

One particular Sunday, perhaps because it was very hot, Bubba had been more restless than usual. When the collection basket had passed above him, he'd tried to wrest it from the usher's hands. During the Sanctus, he'd suddenly taken it into his head to tell the story of "The Little Engine That Could" to an old lady two pews forward. He was still going strong at the Communion, when Pa and Mama had to receive separately, one staying behind to restrain the youngster while the other darted up the aisle and back again.

"I think I can...I think I can..." Lyman Gene cried, as the chalice was returned to the tabernacle. His father gripped his shoulders and his mother buried her face in her hands. "Mercy!" whispered a voice behind them.

Perhaps he'd worn himself out, for he appeared to settle down after Communion. Even the rousing last hymn, "Salve, Regina," hadn't been enough to rouse him. After Mass, Monsignor Shea led the rosary in a weary drone. Lyman Gene sat hunched between his parents. He seemed nearly asleep.

Murana, just old enough to be embarrassed by her little brother's carryings-on, breathed a sigh of relief and mumbled the prayers along with the priest.

"Glory be to the Father and to the Son and..."

"Bzzz."

She ignored the sound, tried to pretend she hadn't heard it.

"Bzzz." It grew louder.

She moved on with Monsignor. "...is now and ever shall be..."

"*Bzzz.*" She felt the sharp sting of tiny fingernails pinching her upper arm.

Murana spun around and glared at Lyman. He had slipped across the pew behind Pa and was now next to Murana, grinning and flapping his bent elbows like wings.

"Will you *hush*?"

"Bzzz." His hand, quick as a mouse, darted under the skirt of her organdy dress. The sting landed high on the back of her leg, almost on her fanny.

"Ma!" She said it louder than she meant to and both Clive and Mary Alice looked at her with surprise and disappointment. Bubba, leaning back into the pew, lowered his eyelids and sighed as if disturbed from sleep.

"Our Father, Who art in Heaven, hallowed be..."

"Bzzz."

Murana swatted, hitting her own ear so hard it made her eyes water.

"Ain't no such *thing*!" she'd shouted at him when they got home. "Nossir."

"Stings," Lyman Gene whispered, his bitty fingers flying toward her neck.

She waved him away. "Not *that* kinda bee, silly."

"*Stings!*" His voice filled the Ruckus Room and traveled up the stairs.

"What's all the commotion?" Mary Alice called. "The Angel of Mischief land down there?"

"The *Glory Bee*!" the little boy crowed.

Upstairs, his parents laughed. "Glory be to you, too!" his mother answered.

Lyman looked at Murana with a triumphant grin. "Glory Bee gonna sting you," he said. "All your born days, Murana Bill."

"Quit actin' a fool," his sister said.

"Bzzz," said Bubba.

"Mama . . . Mama . . ."

She was very nearly asleep when she heard him. "Mama!" His voice was hoarse and strangled with grief.

He'd spoken.

Murana was on her feet and halfway up the stairs before it really got through to her: Bubba could talk.

"Mama . . ."

She unbolted his bedroom door. Her legs wobbling, she clutched at the doorframe to keep from sinking to the floor.

He was waiting for her. In his rush to the kitchen, he nearly sent her toppling backward down the steep flight of stairs.

Bent double, clinging to the peaked top of the newel post, Murana listened to the creak of the kitchen's swinging door, in and out, in and out, abbreviating its own motions as it wound down like a top.

"Mama." If he could say that, then he ought to be able to say "Murana," oughtn't he? The sounds were so close alike. But it was Mama he wanted.

Cabinet doors slammed, followed by a clatter of pots and pans. She remembered the saucepan of soup on the stove, perhaps still a little warm. But he'd have eaten that by now. The box of saltines would be long gone.

Her left knee balanced on the cold wooden planks, Murana crouched in the dark hallway, hearing the sounds of her brother's unscrupulous hunger. She lowered her head, pressing her cheek to the smooth grain of the polished oak railing. It was scented with lemon oil, sweet and sharp.

The sun would start up anytime now. Outdoors the birds were creating a sweet chaos, like a symphony orchestra getting in tune.

His voice, in disuse for nearly five years, was still there inside him.

For weeks he refused to look at her. He didn't speak again, and Murana hadn't expected he would. But his refusal to let their eyes meet afflicted her with a sorrow whose like she'd never known.

Murana knew that in the town her life was thought sad. She saw the pity in people's eyes. But all she herself perceived was a life that was normal. A life that had sadness in it, yes, but her sorrows had been natural ones. Parents died. Young men went off to war. Murana accepted her portion of the normal course of events. As far as she could see, the single circumstance which elevated her existence from the plain and ordinary was having Lyman Gene in her care.

Folks had said it was a tragedy, too, when he came home mute from war. Maybe their view was right. Her brother's silence, like the death of her parents, somehow seemed inevitable, though. Natural. Tragedy, as Murana understood it, was something unnatural.

When Lyman Gene stopped looking at her, however, Murana felt true tragedy upon her, and she knew she wasn't equal to it.

Her brother was engaging her in a contest. Even as a small boy, he'd always been able to find her soft spots. The force and cleverness of his will had been clear before he could walk or talk, as if knowing how to get his own way was a sixth sense he was born with.

Opposing him had never appealed to Murana. Instead, she'd taken it upon herself to anticipate his wants. To be able to give something before he asked it was a sort of triumph. And when she failed at that, she worked to make lavish amends.

Strangely, Murana's concessions to her baby brother hadn't always seemed to please her parents. "You got to stand up for your rights once in a while," her father would say, worried love clouding his eyes.

"I declare, you got no will of your own," Mama told her one Christmas night, finding all Murana's new toys in the stenciled chest in Lyman Gene's room.

But Mama had been wrong. Murana did have a will of her own. It was simply identical to her brother's: what he wanted, she wanted for him.

What he wanted now, with an unspoken, blank-eyed fury, was food. More food than a body could possibly need or manage. The food that Doc Purchase said would be the death of him.

And he knew how to get it. To demolish his sister's intentions, he simply withdrew from her. For several years now, she'd had only the calm gray surface of his eyes, receding further and further into folds of flesh, to inform her of his wants and reassure her of his love. She was rewarded and guided solely by his eyes.

When he stopped looking at her, she was lost.

The week after Lyman Gene had stripped the pantry bare, Murana awoke in the middle of the night to the pangs of a potent hunger. Her stomach rumbled and roiled, making noises like amorous cats, and sharp pains assailed her under the breastbone. Her mouth was watering.

She'd left the pantry empty. The icebox, too. Since no precaution could keep him from the food, the only solution was to keep none around. She went to the market three times a day.

Now, however, in the vague endless hours between midnight and dawn, she was starving and there was nothing edible in the house. Even the preserved goods in the cellar were gone: Lyman had discovered them the week before.

Across the hall, she heard him snore, long gasps of effort strung together with short intervals of ease. She got up, stepping unerringly into her slippers, and went to his room.

The dim night-light glowed on his bedside table. Murana didn't know if it comforted him at all—he'd never wanted one as a child—but it consoled her to know that he had it.

The room seemed crowded with overlapping blue shadows, the windows covered with black lace. Murana stood next to his bed, marveling at the measureless depth of her brother's sleep. His stomach, sloping toward the ceiling, lurched under a tangle of blankets with each breath. And as if he meant to reject and reprove her even in sleep, his face was turned to the wall.

She stayed for a long time, watching him as she listened to the muffled howls of hunger which, although they came from inside her, seemed clearly his. They were starving together, without the comfort of so much as a glance between them.

It was a battle, she knew. Very possibly a battle to the death. It could go on for weeks, months. But Murana knew in her famished soul that the outcome was preordained.

She had a will of her own. She would, in the one way possible, restore the only life that was possible, a life that came naturally. And could be borne. And would, she understood, naturally be borne away, beyond her reaching.

Her brother was all she had, and Murana lacked the hard, joyless gumption that was the stuff of tragedy.

6

*I*t was October 1975 when the battle between Lyman Gene and Murana Bill began, starting with the rout in the kitchen pantry. Six weeks went by, days of terrible deprivation, cold and hunger beyond imagining.

Lyman Gene retreated into sleep, as if his dreams provided clandestine nourishment, forbidden delicacies. He woke only to consume the beautiful meager meals his sister carried into his room on trays three times each day.

He ate in bed, his eyes lowered grimly to bowls of lettuce, plates of lean broiled meat, amorphous soft-boiled eggs already scooped from their shells into chaste glass custard cups. The sheets of his bed were littered with unbuttered toast crumbs, his filthy pajamas stained with tomato juice and greenish soups.

Murana would stand in the hallway outside his room and watch him eat. No matter how near she came, Lyman Gene refused to acknowledge her presence by so much as a glance. So, fiercely hungry, she lurked at his door like a beggar. She rarely ate herself—only when she began to grow faint. It seemed somehow essential that she deny herself more than she denied him.

And he denied her completely. The moment he finished eating, he'd lean over the edge of the bed to set his empty tray on the floor. Then he'd roll over to face the wall, falling into a deep sleep again.

By November, Murana was failing fast. If Lyman Gene was losing weight, it wasn't apparent: there was simply too much of him for small losses or gains to register. But his sister was wasting away. She looked ghostly. Her dry skin had the yellowish tinge of an ancient lampshade so perishable a human finger might poke holes in it. Even her large, angular bones appeared reduced. Her hair came out in handfuls when she brushed it in the morning.

On the first of November, All Saints' Day, a Jesuit priest from Berea came to Mount Vadalia to offer a solemn High Mass in the little storefront church. Mass on a weekday at five o'clock in the afternoon seemed a marvelous luxury to Murana. She fixed supper, vegetable soup and a fruit salad, early in the day. Lyman Gene rarely came downstairs anymore, anyway. And if he did? Well, he'd just be having his supper early, then.

At ten minutes to five, after looking in on her dozing brother, she quietly left the house and walked up the street toward the church. It was already growing dark, but the air was surprisingly warm. In the west, swirls of light the color of peach jam were daubed along the horizon.

She slipped into the church, taking a seat behind a fair-sized man in a plaid knit sport coat: Riley McCue. Murana bowed her head, suddenly so tired. She imagined herself in a great cathedral, an elaborate black-shadowed cavern in some foreign country. She saw her own body stretched out on a pink-and-gray marble floor, felt its smooth chill against her forehead and through the coarse linen of her white robe. The air would be heavy with incense and dying flowers and chanting..."Prostrate." She remembered the word from some prayer or other. "I shall prostrate myself at the foot of Thy altar." It sounded so restful, like a complete letting-go...laying down all the soul's troubles in front of the Lord and just leaving them there.

Perhaps she fell asleep for a moment, entangled in her peaceful, purifying dream. Next thing she knew, the voice of the priest was reciting the Confiteor: "I confess to Almighty God, and to you my brothers and sisters, that I have sinned through my own fault..."

Murana lifted her head and looked around. Beside her, Peggy Anne Sligo, her hair covered with a bright woolen scarf, was studying her with a sneaky worried look. The thick lenses of her glasses were filmed with chalk dust.

"In what I have done, and in what I have failed to do," Murana murmured, with a reassuring smile to Peggy Anne."

The visiting priest, Father Albamonti, devoted his sermon to joy. Joy, he said, was God's first true reason for creating man... only because of Adam and Eve, there had to be suffering, too. But the Lord wanted His people to live their earthly lives serving Him with as much gladness as possible, and then to know joy everlasting with Him in heaven.

And All Saints' Day, he said, was a festival of joy, like a great birthday party honoring all those already enjoying God's heavenly gladness.

Murana sat in the small, drafty church, half-listening. She pictured a gigantic cake covered with seven-minute icing, its tiny candles like a galaxy of stars. All Saints: Clement, Cletus, Cornelius, Cosmas, Cyprian, Cecilia... as a child she'd known a whole long list by heart, from a part of the Mass they didn't say out loud anymore. Thaddeus. Sixtus. Damian. She wondered what had happened to all those saints, whether the Holy Father took some of them off the list like he did to Saint Christopher...

"Tomorrow," Father Albamonti said, "we observe the Feast of All Souls, remembering the faithful departed. And yesterday, the little children Jesus so loves celebrated Halloween. All Hallows' Eve—hallow means holy. All souls have the capacity for holiness. This means that all *souls* are potentially all *saints*..."

Murana closed her eyes again. She didn't feel like a saint.

She could barely remember gladness. She wondered, with a bitterness that frightened and shamed her, why God, having given her the gift of her brother, refused to show her how to care for him. If gladness was what He was after, why did He make such a mighty misery over such a puny and ordinary thing as an apple? Why couldn't He have just stomped His Almighty foot on the head of that snake and have done with it?

Halloween was a holiday Murana loved nearly as well as Christmas. For a full week beforehand, she'd bake cookies and cupcakes, icing them in orange and cocoa, dotting them with gumdrops and chocolate sprinkles to make witches and jack-o'-lanterns and cats with arched backs and stand-up tails. When it began to get dark, she'd turn out all the lights in the front part of the house, light a few candles in the vestibule and sit waiting for the neighbors' children, a raggedy sheet with two eyeholes draped over her head. When the doorbell rang, she'd feel her mouth stretching out in a grin, her lips not even trying to cover those teeth of hers. For Halloween, Murana wore a no-holds-barred smile of gladness.

The children loved her as a ghost, much more than when they saw her as herself. She knew how to scare the little ones just a little, the older ones out of their wits. She looked forward to Halloween for the whole rest of the year.

But yesterday at dusk she'd turned off all the lights and without lighting any candles she'd gone up to her room.

Cookies and cupcakes wouldn't do this year, of course. She had to see to Lyman Gene, do what was best for him. She'd lain across her bed, listening to the sound of his TV. The news came on. That would mean he was asleep. She'd given him supper early. He might not wake up again until morning.

Downstairs the doorbell rang. And rang. The soft musical chimes wouldn't wake him. Murana had stayed on her bed, in the dark, until a quarter to nine, when the ringing finally stopped. In the morning, going out for the breakfast groceries, she found the two crabapple trees in the front yard festooned with pink toilet paper. She wondered if the children would ever like her again.

"Lord, I am not worthy to receive You, but only say the word and I shall be healed."

Murana considered whether it would be a sin to go to Communion with so much bitterness in her heart.

"Only say the word," she prayed, following Riley McCue's broad plaid back up the aisle. Her eyes yearned toward the tabernacle, almost exactly where her father's cash register used to be.

That night, when she took her brother's supper tray up to him, a saucer beside his juice glass held two jack-o'-lantern cookies with candy corn eyes and teeth.

Lyman Gene ate them. But he didn't look at her.

And so he got his way, just as she'd known he would.

It took near a month to win him back. She wooed him with mashed potatoes and pineapple fritters and sticky buns. She negotiated in butter, sugar, and flour, surrendered with cakes and pies in her outstretched hands. Because she had to go to the store alone and on foot, she couldn't refill the refrigerator and restock the pantry overnight, but she tried. And it did seem that each day she was able to carry a little more weight in the brown paper bags from Purdy's Market.

At night, after dinner, she made hot chocolate and popcorn. She filled the carnival glass candy dish in the parlor with sour balls and red-hots and peppermints, and went out before breakfast for fresh doughnuts. Gradually, her days took on a tentative sort of pleasure again, for she knew it was only a matter of time before her brother would come around.

. . . .

Thanksgiving marked the end of hostilities.

Early that week, with the help of Coach Comstock, Murana borrowed an aluminum folding table from the high-school gym and mapped out a regular banquet to be held in Lyman Gene's room. She even went to the bank and asked Mr. Moody to retrieve Mama's good sterling from the vault.

"Having a party, are you?" he asked.

Murana smiled shyly. "Just family," she said, as if there could be something more.

On Thanksgiving Day, she was in and out of her brother's room all morning, setting things up. A delicate cross-stitched cloth and napkins and a battery of crystal and silver serving pieces were carried in and meticulously placed. Thin-stemmed goblets. Hand-painted dessert plates.

Tiny blue glass saltcellars in filigree baskets. It filled Murana with an aching kind of joy to see and touch the fine things Mama had used on family holidays. The centerpiece was a cornucopia, spilling over with grapes and tangerines and walnuts whose shells were brushed with gilt.

As Murana labored over the feast, her brother remained in bed, covers pulled up to his chin, eyes closed. But several times when she seemed to be paying him no mind, she noticed him watching her.

At twelve-thirty, changed into her good navy wool dress with a dotted scarf anchored at the neck by Mama's majolica brooch, Murana began carrying covered silver dishes and cut-glass bowls up the stairs. Lyman Gene pretended to sleep.

Then Murana was standing over him, gently prodding his shoulder. "Bubba?"

He opened his eyes, looking out the window behind her.

"Well, I'll just go and get the bird," she said. Her smile was as coy as a young girl's.

When she returned, staggering under the weight of a twenty-pound turkey on a footed silver platter, Lyman Gene was at the table. His hair was wetted down and freshly combed.

She set the turkey in front of her brother and placed a set

of bone-handled carving utensils at his right hand.

Lyman Gene looked from one end of the table to the other. Tufts of steam hovered above a dozen dishes. Curls of sweet butter lay on a bed of shaved ice.

"Shall we say grace?"

Lyman Gene lifted his eyes to meet his sister's, and smiled.

By Christmas week, Murana had some color again. She slept through the night, unless Lyman Gene woke her in his hungry travels down the stairs. She fretted less. "He is a bit stout," she admitted to herself, "but at least he's happy."

Murana meant for this to be a very special Christmas. At the market she bought magazines full of unusual holiday recipes and gifts you could make from things around the house. She started on a wreath for the McCues—a frame made of coat-hangers covered with candies wrapped in cellophane. But when it was half-finished, she came downstairs one morning and found a bare wire ring, misshapen, and little wads of cellophane scattered across the kitchen table. She tried to scold Lyman, but wound up laughing: he looked at her with such innocence.

As a surprise she was making him a new bathrobe. Mr. Willis had sent to Cincinnati for 100 percent cashmere cloth: $31.95 a yard, and it was going to take more yards than she cared to think about. The robe would be pale gray, with lapels like the tuxedo jacket Pa used to wear to the Rotary Christmas Dinner-Dance. Rich maroon silk cording would edge the lapels and belt. Murana's stitching had never been more close to perfect. Now Bubba would be able to dress up for special occasions.

His second present, though, would be even grander. Months ago, in early fall, Murana had given the photograph of Lyman Gene in his army uniform to Peggy Anne, who'd been working ever since on a copy in oils. The portrait would surely be beautiful, framed in silver, with a black velour border that looked like velvet but would hold up better, Peggy Anne said. It would hang above the parlor mantelpiece, replacing the print of *My Old Kentucky Home* that Pa bought Mama on a trip to Bardstown. That could go in the hall.

A few days before Christmas, Glenda McCue stopped by with gifts: a two-pound sack of Georgia pecans, a brandy snifter filled with homemade bourbon balls, Avon cologne in a kitten-shaped bottle for Murana, and soap-on-a-rope for Lyman Gene.

Murana opened all the packages right away, even her brother's.

"Why, isn't that the cunningest thing?" She swung the soap alongside her knees, jerking the cord a little, like a yo-yo.

Glenda smiled. "How is Lyman Gene?" she asked.

"He's the best boy in creation," Murana said. "Don't give us a lick of trouble."

"We'd surely love to see him one of these days, Riley and me."

"And wouldn't he just love to see you, too." The edges of Murana's teeth showed briefly, her lips turning back in a cautious smile. "Now, tell me what-all you'll be doing for Christmas."

"I'm trying a goose this year—can you stand it?"

"A goose!" Murana cried. "Now that's a thing I'd love to sample. Bubba's devoted to my country ham, though."

"Why don't you come, the both of you? Riley could call for you..."

"You're sweet as can be! But you know how things are..."

Glenda, who didn't know but was trying to figure it out, said, "Sure, honey. Course we do."

"A goose," Murana said. "My, oh, me! I wish I was creative like that. I did make us a plum pudding one year but can't rightly say I thought too highly of it."

"Like soggy fruitcake," Glenda agreed. "You'll be stayin'

home, then, I guess? Just the two of you?"

"Two peas in a pod."

Murana tried to overlook the pity in Glenda McCue's expression . . . and something else. Disapproval, she thought.

"Why don't you come to us," she said. "On Christmas Eve? Bubba'd be just tickled to see you."

"We're going *where*?!" Riley McCue bellowed.

"Yes, indeedy. Mr. and Miss Bill has requested the pleasure—the considerable pleasure, I might say—of our company at a Christmas Eve soi-ree."

"We always stay home Christmas Eve."

"It's a act of pure Christian charity to go," Glenda said. "Besides, what better way to find out what's going on over there?"

"Aw, honey . . ."

"Ooh, *honey!*" She swatted him on the seat of the pants, knowing the quickest route to his heart.

"Why, my brother's not hardly well enough to be going out in the cold, I say. But here's an idea—why don't you come to us? I swear, I didn't know what was in my head till it popped right outa my mouth that way. But then, besides that it's already too late once it's said, I'm thinking to myself, girl, these folks been so *good* . . . all them rides 'fore we had the church here, you know, while you was gone. Seems like a long time ago, don't it? And coming by here in all kinda weather just to look in on us and make sure we're getting along. Bubba, I can't remember a single solitary time I seen neither one when practically the first word outa their mouth ain't, 'Murana, how's that fine young man who's your brother?'

"Well, having them over's the least we can do . . ."

Lyman Gene lay on his back in the bed, his head propped

up with three pillows. His eyes were riveted on his sister's face.

"So I guess we're having us a party, Bubba," she said, clapping her hands softly together. "Won't that be grand?"

Pallid and pudgy as bratwurst, his fingers groped in the drawer of his nightstand and came out with a handful of Hershey Kisses. With practiced fingers he began to peel away the silver foil and pop the candies, one after the other, into his round pink mouth. All the while, he never stopped gazing blankly at his sister's flushed face.

"Don't go spoiling your supper now," she said, patting the soft slab of his cheek.

Lyman Gene parted his lips and gave her a wet chocolaty grin.

"I just knew you'd be tickled," she said.

Christmas Eve morning, Murana was putting the last of the wine-colored cording to Lyman Gene's robe when Starbuck Sligo, Peggy Anne's brother, came by to drop off the portrait. Seeing the Sligos' old black pickup from the front parlor window, Murana let the heap of gray cashmere slide to the floor and ran out to the hallway with a tin of Christmas cookies and a dollar for the boy.

The picture was wrapped in fresh brown paper and tied with twine. She couldn't wait to see it. But she had to make sure about Bubba first. She tiptoed up the stairs and peeked in on him. He was fast asleep.

The twine was so tightly and intricately knotted she needed a kitchen knife to get it off. Though she usually saved paper for reusing, she didn't bother this time. She tore the sheets away, and there he was.

Murana hadn't laid eyes on the photograph since September, when she'd turned it over to Peggy Anne. Now it fell to the floor, facedown among the wrappings, but she didn't have to turn it over to see the likeness. Even the world globe behind him was exact—the United States with the little yellow tail that was Florida, and all of South America below it, dark pink and shaped like a ham.

Beneath the bill of his cap, her brother's eyes were the same soft gray of the Persian lamb collar on Mama's best coat. They shone with a light that seemed to come from deep inside, from his very soul, Murana thought. She sat down on the piano bench, the breath quite knocked out of her by her brother's handsomeness.

He looked a bit different now, of course. Older, and not so lean. Come to think of it, he'd been altogether too thin back then, too slight a boy to be fighting a jungle war in borrowed clothes.

Murana hung the picture over the mantel and covered it with a clean white sheet, folded in quarters. The scent of lavender sachet lingered in the parlor for a moment before it was absorbed by the stronger fragrance of the pine Christmas tree.

Murana examined the white-draped rectangle on the wall. There was something mournful about it, reminding her how she'd read that in some religion or other folks would cover all the mirrors in a house when somebody died. Shivering, she snatched the sheet away to look into her brother's lovely gray eyes again. Yes, there was Lyman Gene, safe and sound. Around him the silver frame glistened in the cold winter sunshine, almost blinding against the rich black matte.

When Murana finally covered the portrait, she fastened sprigs of holly and crepe myrtle to the sheet corners and pinned a large red satin bow in the center.

It looked downright festive that way, she thought.

At half-past seven, silver compote dishes of cookies and candy, platters of cake, and the monstrous cut-glass punch bowl of eggnog were waiting on the dining room sideboard. Candles flickered everywhere; with the winking colored lights on the tree, and a fire, there was hardly any need for lamps. Murana put a record on the phonograph in the cellar, *Perry Como's Christmas Favorites*, and turned it up loud enough to carry upstairs.

"Wouldn't Mama love to be here?" She was getting Lyman situated in a wingback chair, where he could look at the tree. She set a plate of cookies beside him on a cherry candlestand.

"Now don't go tampering in the dining room before company comes. Pa, too—yes, surely. They did love a good Christmas near about as much as anything in this world."

Lyman Gene blinked.

"Your new robe just suits you...reminds me of Ronald Colman in one of them old romance movies Mama'd be moonin' over. Why, you oughta have you a butler and maid, Bubba, not just a raggedy old sister seein' to you."

He groped for the cookies, still watching her.

"Seems like somethin's missing yet, though...wait!"

She dashed up the stairs, returning in a moment with a long white silk scarf of Mama's. She wrapped it around her brother's massive neck, tucking the fringed ends inside the lapels of his robe.

"You are a glory," she said.

The doorbell rang. As Murana went to answer it, Lyman Gene transferred the plate of cookies to his lap.

A nimbus of frozen air radiated from the McCues' bundled forms as Murana herded them into the parlor. Their cheeks were red, their noisy greetings laced with hot buttered rum.

"Now you just hand me them coats and get yourself over by the fire," Murana said. "Bubba, you remember Mr. and Miz...Glenda and Riley?" She paused, beaming as if the others were embracing.

Riley handed her a liquor bottle in a striped foil bag. "Ho-ho-ho," he said.

She turned to his wife. "Well, ain't he just a card?"

"How are you, hon?" Glenda kissed her.

Crossing the room, duty-bound and manly, Riley held out his hand to Lyman Gene. "Good to see you, boy."

Looking to his sister, Lyman covered his plate of cookies with splayed fingers.

"Bubba could hardly wait to see you. Why, your comin' by just *makes* our Christmas."

"Wouldn't miss it for the world," Riley said, backing away from Lyman Gene.

"Not for the world," his wife echoed. "Rile's barely stopped talking about it for the past few days."

With a frantic sort of pleasure, Murana goaded her guests toward the food and drink. "I wish you'd of come for a real supper, though."

"Well, this *is* a supper, I'd say ... I can feel it on my hips already!" Then Glenda blushed, having sworn to her husband only minutes before that she'd steer clear of the subject of diets. "I gotta watch it at my age," she whispered, winking at Murana.

When they returned to the parlor, carrying loaded plates, Lyman had finished his cookies and was working his way through a dish of divinity. Bits of candied cherry, caught in his teeth, shone.

The McCues sat down close together on the settee. Murana remained standing in front of the fireplace, her hands fidgeting. Finally, she cleared her throat, like someone preparing to give a speech.

"Seems like Santy's been by here," she said. "Turns out he had a very special somethin' for this house in that bag of his."

Bashfully, she turned around to face the mantel. "'Now, Miss Murana,' Santy said, 'might be your friends the Riley McCues gonna think you got some mighty peculiar artwork hangin' in your parlor. But never you mind. I want you to do just like I say. 'Cause what I got here ain't no ordinary present.

And it's for that sweet brother of yours.'"

Clumsily, she pulled the bed sheet down, whipping it back with a flourish that fanned the flames of the fire. Ashes rose like a swarm of pale mosquitoes and were drawn up the flue.

Behind her there was silence.

Murana longed to turn around, to watch her brother's face. For weeks and weeks she'd been dreaming of the surprised gladness and awakened love she'd find...

In fact, she'd even made up a story about it, how the beautiful picture would beckon back Lyman Gene's old self: the block of frozen-solid secrets in his throat would melt, freeing his voice, and he'd call out her name with a whoop and holler of wild joy...

The silence at her back seemed endless, a sweep of time and distance beyond reckoning or recovery. Murana couldn't turn around to face it. Her eyes seemed eternally condemned to look at the portrait...

That awful picture.

Fancied up, it was still the same, a falsehood and a forgery. Below the silver edge of the frame, she knew, he didn't have any pants on. The jacket and billed cap were a costume, photographer's props, and the light in his eyes was only a trick of Peggy Anne's paintbrush.

Murana turned and looked across the parlor at her brother. Then she glanced back at the picture. That was no hero up there, only a boy. And the boy was long gone.

Riley McCue whistled. "Well, if that ain't a likeness to end all," he said.

Grunting softly, Lyman Gene hoisted himself from his chair and lumbered through the dining room door.

7

"Now, you just go ahead and cry," folks said, as they came through the front parlor of the Fern Brothers' Funeral Home to press her hands and shake their heads at the stern wonder of death.

"Sorry for your trouble."

"Bless your heart."

"Don't he look fine, though?"

"The Lord works in mysterious ways."

Murana Bill straightened her spine, smoothing the skirt of her black double-knit dress over her hips, and said over and over again, "Thank you kindly for coming by." Every few minutes she glanced fondly at the blond wood casket, smiling as if to reassure her dead brother that he was behaving beautifully and she was holding up fine.

The dead man, whose age would have been impossible to guess had everyone in town not already known it, weighed four hundred and twenty-three pounds. He was attired, for this last great occasion of his existence, in a gray cashmere robe piped in deep red. A white silk scarf was loosely knotted at his throat, and a string of tiger's-eye rosary beads was entwined through his stiff and swollen-looking fingers. Mr. Billy Fern seemed to have got carried away with his well-known artistry: the lips of the deceased were tinged with mauve, and he appeared to be blushing, as if uncomfortable with all the attention.

Against all odds, his heart had held out for five more years, years that for his sister were an unquestioning blur of joy and necessity. "Why" was a word that hardly occurred to her. "How" had been given its answers with the passing of time. She saw to him. And he was everything to her.

Lyman Gene Bill died in April, on a night when rain softly pelted the windows and dripped steadily from the eaves. His sister never heard him leaving her. Only in the sun-spotted morning, when she walked into his room carrying his breakfast tray, did she come to find him gone.

He was curled up on his side, his fingers bent toward his mouth as if he'd just stopped sucking on them. His eyes were open as usual, big baby eyes that would latch onto her first thing, wide and gray and greedy.

When his eyes stayed put, fastened on the dogwood branches framed in his window, Murana knew before she got one foot through the door that her brother was gone. That this time he wouldn't be given back. Her life was fresh out of miracles.

She sat down on the edge of the mattress, not touching him, and looked into his eyes. They were clear and peaceful, a boy's eyes, but without the curiosity of boyhood. She didn't see the mottled skin at his throat, a rash, nor the stubble on his chin. She was blind to the thinness of his hair and the grotesque rolls of fat which had come to encase and define every inch of him. She saw only his eyes, and they seemed to her, even dulled by death, so full of promise.

The night-light was still burning, weak and myopic among dusty sunbeams. Murana reached over to the bedside table and flicked it off. Then she took her brother in her arms, pushing her flattened hand and wrist hard against the mattress to get them wedged under him. She tried to raise his head and shoulders to take a part of him in her lap, but his weight defeated her. Finally, she slipped down to rest beside him.

She stayed there for a very long time, her head next to his on the pillow. Pinned beneath him, her left hand was numb; the other lay palm down on the still slope of his shoulder.

When the sun was high in the sky, Murana pulled herself away from her brother and rose. The air in the room had grown hot and stale. She opened the windows wide, letting in a breeze and the sound of birds.

Murana soaked a washcloth in rosewater and bathed her brother's face and neck and hands. His nails were bitten to the quick, so far down in some places that they'd bled. His fingers felt soft and formless, as if the bones had been removed from them. Tenderly, she scrubbed between them, not missing a spot. Then she held the cool cloth to his cooler forehead, the way she'd done when he got feverish as a child.

The April air, but for the sunshine, was deceptively chilly. A bee was bouncing angrily against the screen. Early, Murana thought. Well before summer still. She shut the windows. Then she took the gray cashmere robe and covered her brother with it, before going downstairs to call Doc Purchase.

"He looks grand," folks said. "Simply grand."

The air in Viewing Parlor II was florid with carnations and roses. Sneaking a smoke in the parking lot out back, leaning on the bumper of an ancient limousine, several of the gentlemen callers speculated how the lid of that coffin in there was going to get closed with the great gray mound of belly sticking up like it was.

"Turn him on his side, I reckon."

"Don't hardly matter, now, does it?"

"Ain't he a sight?"

"Don't look like no hero *I* ever seen."

Inside, in the parlor, their wives whispered to the bereaved sister, sole survivor, "Grand . . . don't he look peaceful, though?" And, "You call on us now, if there's anything you need."

Folks talked about it later: how all through the funeral, even at the cemetery, Murana Bill never shed a tear. When Lyman Gene was lowered into the ground with a groan of ropes and pulleys, Mr. Bobby Fern, Jr., stepped smartly forward to grasp her elbow and offer his handkerchief, as if prompting her with an important piece of business. Murana looked delicately away, her dry eyes coming to rest on a standing pyramid of red and white gladioli. A small American flag shot out from its center: her brother was a Veteran of Foreign Wars.

The whole town, not large enough to be stratified or fragmented, had turned out for the funeral, and Murana Bill's composure came as a disappointment and a shock. Mount Vadalia had known her for all thirty years of her life, a softhearted Kentucky girl whose eyes would swim at a puppy's limp, a choir's vibrato, a passing parade. So it would be only natural that the death of her brother, her last living kin, should bring her low. The town meant to brace her.

But Murana Bill was letting them down. Her firm chin and set shoulders and unclouded gaze left folks feeling useless, awkward, even scandalized. She didn't flinch when the volley of shots was fired over the cemetery wall. She accepted the tightly triangulated flag with a queenly self-possession, as if she had ceremonial chores to perform every day. The mourners scattered to their cars in confusion, like a platoon of foot soldiers deprived of command.

"Ain't hardly natural," Glenda McCue told her husband, as they followed a line of cars to the Bill home for the post-funeral spread.

"It's a shock." As the town's only authorized automobile dealer (Mountain Motors Chrysler-Plymouth), Riley McCue was something of an expert in the ways of human crisis. "Just give the poor gal time."

As often happened, Riley McCue was right on the money. A scant hour later, while she unmolded a pineapple-lime gelatin ring in the pantry, Murana Bill went completely to pieces.

Her wails of anguish and despair, carrying through the dining room and parlor to the front porch where her neighbors waited for a call to the buffet, caused considerable relief. The women exchanged satisfied, wise looks and began working their way toward the back of the house. The men stared at their hands, or off in the distance, or into their little plastic glasses of fruit punch. Out back, at the far edge of the yard, the children, playing Mother-May-I beside the Rushing Milk River, paused, inclining their heads toward the unfamiliar sounds of adult misery and terror.

Father Etienne Armand had been sent from the Benedictine retreat house near Hazard to officiate at the funeral. Such assignments appalled him, for he knew he was unequal to human suffering. Contemplation was his true métier.

Now, hearing the cries of immediate need from the kitchen, the young priest glanced hungrily at the greening springtime hills. For an all-too-human instant, he prayed for this cup to pass. Monsignor Shea from St. Boniface knew the bereaved, after all. If only the old man's gall bladder had not chosen this particular week...

Father Armand envisioned himself hiking up the hem of his cassock and ascending the slope until he was beyond the sight or touch of mortal grieving, wrapped in soundless white clouds. Then hearing the splash of the overfilled river behind the house, he recalled his temporary shepherd's duties. In the wake of the women, he entered the vale of tears.

Miss Murana Bill was collapsed at the kitchen table, a sturdy slab of oak. Her head was cradled in her arms, and as she rocked back and forth, her bones made a grinding sound against the worn seat of a pressback chair.

The older women encircled her, murmuring and patting her clothes. The younger women fanned out from the sides of this crowded Pietà. Wide-eyed and silent, a group of girls clustered in the doorway, where the priest joined them.

"O Lord," Murana wept. "Lord a mighty."

"He was all she had," said a woman with a crown of iron-colored plaits, looking at Father Armand over Murana's crumbled back. "All she had in this living world."

Murana raised her head and stared past Father Armand toward the pantry, where peridot-hued gelatin was beginning to melt off the edges of a hobnailed glass cake-plate. "What on earth will I do?" she whispered.

A woman in a gray felt jumper crossed swiftly to the pantry and removed the gelatin to the freezer. "Firm her right up," she said. Another rummaged in the cabinet below the sink. In a moment, she found what she was looking for: a bottle of ammonia. She splashed some on the corner of a clean white dish towel and held it under Murana's nose.

"Everything's gonna be fine, honey."

"Amen," muttered Mrs. Aileen Timmons, organist for the Calvary Hill Third Baptist Church. Then she gave the Catholic priest a sheepish look.

Several of the older women nodded vehemently.

"Just fine. You'll see."

Murana's head reared back. Her nostrils flared, and only the whites of her eyes showed. With her prominent teeth bared, her long narrow face twitching, she reminded Father Armand of the wild ponies he'd seen as a boy in Alberta.

I have no place here, he thought.

"He was all she had," Mrs. Timmons cried.

"Amen," the priest murmured, backing out of the kitchen and leaving the women to their lay mission.

"That ought to do it," someone said.

*T*raveling down a road, off in the country somewhere, you're apt to come upon a simple thing, something that might stop you cold if you'd only pause and consider it. But chances are you won't. A single shoe or boot has come to be as common a sight on the roadside as milkweed, say, or a cola can. Nobody much wonders how they come to be there.

Murana was less than an hour out of Mount Vadalia, coming onto the Mountain Parkway. She took the curved ramp at twenty-five miles per hour, even though the sign said forty. That was when she saw it: a perfectly good man's lace-up boot, lying on the edge of the road near a clump of bygone goldenrod.

She didn't get the chance to examine it. She had to concentrate on merging, accelerating, shifting, using her turn signal. But its details lodged in her memory so that she could recall them when it was miles behind: extremely large, brown leather with a rawhide lace and a corrugated sole of reddish rubber. How that boot came to be there, all alone on the shoulder of the road, was something she'd surely have liked to know.

A sign, she thought. Trouble as sure as I'm born. But she didn't mean for herself. She was setting off on a new venture to a strange land, right enough. But what trouble could come of it? All she'd meant to keep was already gone. She was heading for Louisville without a thing to lose.

Who lost that boot, though? How? And why? It saddened her to ponder the possibilities. One fine boot, lost or lying abandoned along the road, seemed to her a symbol of all the sorrow and trouble and wrongheadedness a body could succumb to. She imagined some poor soul wandering around with one naked foot, the quest leaving cuts and blisters on his heel and dirt between his toes.

There was something downright sinister about it, too. Why, there might be *toes* inside. For if a man could lose his shoe, what else mightn't have been torn from him? She recalled Father Damien and the lepers, whose toes would fall clean off. She read about it in a book when she was a child and still dreamed of it sometimes: her own toes dropping smack to the floor one night when she pulled her stockings off. The awful vision hung over her all the way to Louisville, reminding her that maybe she had a few things left to lose, after all.

Nearly six months her brother Lyman Gene was gone. Bubba. The cry for him still filled her head with a sharp keening. But that was where she kept her grieving, mostly: inside.

On the outside, however, Murana Bill had surprised everybody by becoming an entirely different person. From the day her brother passed on, she seemed to shed her predictability like an old snakeskin, doing all the last things folks expected of her:

She sold her parents' house, first off, to some people from New York City. The man was building a factory just outside of town. Small machine parts, she heard, but nobody seemed to know what for. The woman was writing a book about them old-time Shakers over to Pleasant Hill. She was broad-faced and serious-looking, in spite of the odd clothes she wore: bib overalls and the top of a man's union suit and all sorts of jewelry made from rope and wooden spools. The way she talked, though, fast and sharp and bold, Murana had to suppose she really was a city woman, never mind how she looked.

After the house itself was sold, Murana—without consulting anbody, not even the Riley McCues or Mr. L. T. Moody—called in an auctioneer from Hazard and sold nearly everything in it. She kept only a few things for herself: her own bed and bureau, the parlor settee, the kitchen table Pa's pa had made. The portrait of Lyman Gene. And the Hosanna Quilt, of course.

She'd finished the quilt, finally, in the weeks after Bubba died. Nights when she couldn't sleep, she bent over it as if the work could fend off sorrow, repair memory. Finished, it was astonishingly beautiful. Almost every inch was covered with her own stitching. But Murana still thought of the quilt as something Mama had made, an heirloom passed into her safekeeping.

The auctioneer, licking his lips anxiously and telling jokes Murana couldn't get the gist of, hauled off the whole rest of the load the very day he came to look. He paid a cash sum Murana's neighbors swore was "a steal"—though no one was able to say just how much it was.

That had been in June, so Murana spent her last months in Mount Vadalia in a house that was all but empty. She packed her brother's clothes, so few, and sent them to the Old Soldiers Home in Lexington. She gave half her own to the Boosters Club at the high school for their autumn rummage sale. They were pleased to take cartons of knickknacks and books and such off her hands, too. Murana kept the cuckoo clock, and boxed Mama's collection of carnival glass for Glenda McCue, who'd always had an eye for it. The soda fountain in the basement she left just like it was, stocked and equipped, thinking it would make a nice surprise for the New York couple. They'd probably like the old tools down there, too.

It struck Murana as curious and quite wonderful how stripping down the house seemed to clear room for things she'd lived with her whole life without much noticing—the different way the light fell askance through each window, how sway-backed the floor in the parlor was. And the gentle noises of the river—sometimes like birds or glass bells, sometimes no more than mimicry of a breeze—changing from hour to hour.

The Rushing Milk River, how lovely and mysterious it really was, she realized now. And there it had been, a short jump from the back door, since the day she was born. But how often had she listened to it? Why, she'd scarcely even bothered calling it by its right name. To her and Bubba it was just "the crick." Now she was sorry. She hoped the New York people, seeing it new, learning its name, would pay more heed to what they'd have right beside them.

So the bared house left room for regrets, surely, a whole pack of them. Leavetaking was not a simple task. But even in sorrow, Murana felt something coming together inside her, something brand-new and brave and strong. She concentrated on that, did what it told her needed doing, and tried to look back over her shoulder no more than she had to.

Finally, around about July, when the house scarcely looked like the Bills' place anymore, Murana dropped in on Riley McCue in his office off the showroom of Mountain Motors one blazing afternoon.

The word was all over Mount Vadalia by suppertime: how, within a single hour, Miss Murana Bill had—paying cash, mind you—bought herself a car, complete with the lessons to learn how to drive it.

The car was a Plymouth Fury, almost ten years old, with a ridged black vinyl roof and black leatherette seats. Its flanks were a cool metallic blue, with only a few tiny scratches.

"Somebody took right good care of this baby," Riley McCue said. "Only got sixty thousand on her." Experience had taught him lady customers got a mite squeamish when it came to buying dead folks' cars, so why draw attention?

Murana knew exactly who "somebody" was: Miss Belle Kinney, the retired home ec teacher who'd passed on right behind Lyman Gene. But she put up no fuss. The car suited her to a tee.

Riley felt a mite squeamish himself, though, when his prospect asked him blandly what "four on the floor" meant. Kinda like sending a pretty little orphan child into an unfit home, he thought, looking Murana over for an instant with a jaded eye. Well, she'd learn...

Sixty thousand *what?* Murana wondered.

She couldn't imagine herself driving, even when she was doing it. She had to be very careful not to let her mind wander back a step and picture her behind the wheel, steering and stepping on the brake and clutch and gas pedal. Once that happened, she got all mixed up and scared to death. It reminded her how you couldn't think about your own walking, because if you did, you'd stumble or lose your balance. Breathing was like that, too: didn't work right when you paid attention to it. A body seemed to like being kind of secretive about how it did things.

Before she figured this out, the driving lessons were a misery. Her teacher was Starbuck Sligo, Peggy Anne's brother, who worked as a part-time mechanic for Riley McCue. He was a reliable boy, passionately in love with cars and needing money for the romance: he was rebuilding a '54 Thunderbird convertible almost from scratch. Murana was willing to pay him five dollars an hour for as long as it took her to learn to drive.

It seemed, at first, that it would take forever. Three afternoons a week, tense and sweating and mostly silent, she and Starbuck would veer and jolt down River Street, aiming for the roads outside town which didn't carry much traffic. The car wasn't air-conditioned and even with all four windows rolled down, the heat inside was awful. They might have been roped in hell with seat belts.

In town they were a spectacle. The sight of the blue Fury weaving past made people grin. It got so Starbuck hated going to work, the other boys in the garage were so full of wisecracks about his afternoon "courting" with Miss Murana. But then five dollars an hour, he figured, covered a little guff. She— the T-Bird—was worth it.

Starbuck had his doubts, though, whether Miss Murana would ever get the hang of it. Seemed like she had a regular gift for doing the wrong thing with a car. She'd hit the gas so hard the Fury would leap and squeal, near sent the both of them through the windshield the way she used a brake. She let the clutch out all at once, and whenever she killed the engine that way, she'd look over at him with a sad kind of concern. "Passed out again," she'd say. "You sure this car ain't takin' sick?" The way she steered, her bony elbows wide and flapping, she might have been operating a wheelbarrow.

Once they got out of town, though, things improved some. Murana stopped trying to watch herself and started to concentrate on feeling out the car. The best place was the parking lot behind the abandoned cheese plant. Starbuck found some old trash barrels at the side of the building and set them up to make a slalom course. When Murana stopped knocking the barrels over regularly, he began teaching her to parallel park. The barrels suffered a good bit before she caught on to that.

But she did, eventually, catch on. And she knew the *Commonwealth of Kentucky Rules of the Road*, the little pamphlet from the Department of Motor Vehicles in Frankfort, by heart. Come August, she was out on the county road. Then the interstate highway—even though they had to drive twenty-seven miles to reach it, Starbuck insisted: merging at fifty-five took practice.

The last Wednesday of August, when Murana drove all the way back from the Mountain Parkway without a single close call and parallel-parked perfectly in front of the five-and-dime at the busiest hour of the afternoon, Starbuck told her it was Graduation Day.

"Just one more lesson?" she said.

"Don't see what for." He'd taken her to get her license the previous week and she'd passed with flying colors, though scoring higher on the writing than the driving. "Ain't another thing I can tell you, ma'am."

"Seems like if I'm having my last lesson I oughta *know* it," Murana said.

He shrugged. "Suit yourself."

"Friday. I'll call for you this time."

The boy turned bright red and even more miserable-looking. "I'll be working."

She smiled. "I'll pull in down to the corner, wait by the firehouse."

On Friday afternoon, Murana drove Starbuck Sligo to the Dairy Queen and treated to banana splits. When they'd finished, sitting in the car, she took a small, brightly wrapped package from the glove compartment and handed it to him.

Too bashful to open it in front of her, Starbuck waited until he got home. Under a layer of tissue in the flat box he found a pair of black leather driving gloves with perforated backs and little silver buckles at the wrists. They seemed a bit foolish to him, but he surely didn't feel that way about the twenty-five-dollar bonus check slipped between them. That oughta shut up them boys over to the garage. The gloves mightn't be so bad, either... once he was showing his sweet baby T around town Saturday nights.

At times, Murana was scared half to death by all she didn't know, especially with all she *did* know being sold off, given up, left behind. She wondered how she'd ever be able to explain to folks just what she thought she was doing, when she could barely explain it to herself. She had no earthly notion what she'd be getting into. All she knew for sure was what she had to get out of. She didn't belong in Mount Vadalia anymore, she had no reason to stay. When Bubba died, she became a perfect stranger.

Still, even in the midst of her terrible grief, Murana had begun to get inklings of possibility. The sensation shamed her at first, for it came in little waves that felt oddly like joy, and she figured joy was the last thing she should be feeling. For many years, her one and only job had been seeing to her brother. So when he died, it had not occurred to her that she had any function beyond mourning. She was quiet about it, of course. She held her head up and kept herself busy, seeing to the house, receiving visitors, helping out with the church. Gradually, however, something altogether new, frightening, and quite wonderful began to dawn on her: she had a life.

It was the simplest, most obvious idea in the world. She herself had a life, just like Lyman Gene and Pa and Mama'd had. Murana had never really considered that before. It made her ashamed to catch herself thinking of it now, when she figured she shouldn't have room in her heart for a single thing but sorrow. Still, she received these little hints of hope, of curiosity, of something akin to wonder.

But mostly, something akin to terror. Who would tell her what to do with her earthly days? Where would this life of hers get its shape, its sense of direction, now that she had nobody to tend to? How could she bear to live out these years left to her—whether few or many—as a stranger, a mourner, and nothing more? Yet what else was she fit for?

One Saturday in late June, Monsignor Shea had come over from St. Boniface to hear confessions in Mount Vadalia. Murana, full of doubt and horror at her failings, waited until the tail end of the two hours before she walked into the church.

The tiny, airless confessional—what used to be the lavatory in Pa's store—was hot and black as pitch. Murana thought she might faint. In fact, she wished she would. But right then the warped wood panel shifted aside. Taking a deep breath, she leaned forward (she knew Monsignor was slightly hard of hearing) and spoke into the musty-smelling curtain.

"Bless me, Father, for I have..."

She began to tremble. Her soul, she was sure, wasn't in even the stingiest state of grace. She didn't know where to begin.

"Bless me, Father..." She tried again. "Bless me, I...I can't."

"Take your time," Monsignor whispered. "Do you want to wait a minute, then start again?"

"Yes," Murana said. "I want to start again."

The cubicle was so close, so dark, like the wakeful nights spent wishing the Lord would send for her, have done with it.

"Bless me, Father, for I have..." She began to weep. "I reckon I've near about given up."

The old priest sighed. "Have you a handkerchief?"

"Yessir."

"What is your sin, do you suppose?"

"I don't know what to *do*."

"No sin in that, child."

"Despair?" Murana asked.

"If that were so," the priest said gently, "you wouldn't be here now, would you?"

"I couldn't think where else."

"You did just right, then."

"I am faithless," Murana said.

The monsignor sighed again, and an old-man smell drifted through the curtain. "Is anybody out there?"

"Why, *me*, Father. I am," Murana whispered, indignant.

"Outside, I mean. Waiting for me?"

"No."

"Fine, then. Your penance is to make a good Act of Contrition and go for a walk with me."

Murana drew in a sharp breath, imagining him, this holy man, looking upon her face, knowing who she was and what was in her heart.

"Murana," the priest said softly.

"Yes, it's me," she said.

They walked along in silence for a while, the priest so aged and tired, Murana so disheartened, that neither had to slow down for the other.

"The air's such blessed relief," Monsignor Shea said finally. "That confessional is a step below purgatory this time of year."

Murana blushed. "We ought get you a fan."

"Ah, pay me no mind, girl. Just complainin' to prime the pump."

Monsignor Shea turned his head half in her direction and smiled. Murana was looking down at the cracked pavement. "Still," she said, "I should have thought for your comfort."

"Yours is the comfort that's lacking now, child."

They were outside the center of town, passing by the lumberyard, and the fresh fragrance of green wood filled the air. The pavement ran out after they crossed River Street. They were trampling over tough, dust-nurtured weeds.

Murana stumbled, and the priest steadied her with a hand on her arm. She looked him full in the face then, for the first time. "Reckon I'd feel better if you give me penance," she said. "Comforting's too good for me."

She started to move again, but Monsignor kept hold of her arm and stood still.

"This anger of yours, think it's righteous, do you?" He sounded put out himself.

"Anger? Angry's not what I am, Father."

"Sure and it *is*," the priest snapped. "Only you're sendin' it in the wrong direction, I'd say."

"I don't understand you at all."

This time, when Murana studied him, her eyes had lost their dull look. They were flashing. Ah, yes, indeed she *is* angry, he thought. That's better.

He goaded her. "So I don't know what I'm talkin' about, is that it?"

"I'd never say that, Father."

"But you'd not be above thinkin' it, would you?"

Her eyes filled with tears.

Monsignor Shea began to walk again, still gripping her arm.

"All right," he said. "You give me your account. Tell me this terrible sin of yours."

Murana thought of the sleepless nights of spring, strung together like the harsh icicle-points of light across the Vadalia Palace marquee. Groping and thrashing her way out of nightmares, remembering the emptiness of the room across the hall, she'd tried to foist wild bargains on God, begged to be excused early from her no-account life. After a while, it seemed like being so scared for *herself* didn't hardly leave enough feeling to grieve for Bubba. But what shamed her even more was realizing that, in spite of everything, she harbored a newfound joy. She figured she must be fit for hell, nothing else.

A piecework pickup truck whizzed past, giving a neighborly toot of the horn. Monsignor waved absently, without really looking. "Murana?" he said.

The girl's gaze was off in the hills somewhere. "I can't confess here, in broad daylight," she murmured.

"Confession's over, child. I gave you absolution. But that didn't quite take care of things, did it?"

"Reckon it didn't, no."

"I'm going to tell you something, Murana. Only you must promise me you'll never tell another living soul."

"Yessir?"

"There are some matters a priest may not be equal to. And when that sorry situation arises, I must be something else."

"What—"

The priest laughed quietly. "The shameful fact is, I could never quite bring myself to give up bein' a human being. And if you'll forgive me sayin' so, I'm still mighty good at it, too."

Murana looked at him, bewildered. Her sobriety, her caution were Clive Bill all over, Jeremiah Shea thought.

But suddenly the girl laughed, and the priest recalled Mary Alice Bill, the fresh spirit that had wafted into the rectory with her those many afternoons so long ago.

"Beggin' your pardon, Father." Murana's grin was unguarded, her teeth occupying the better part of her face. "I expect you meant to shock me, but I can't hardly pretend it's somethin' I ain't already noticed myself."

"You don't condemn me?"

"Nossir."

"Mighty understandin' of you." The priest's face grew serious. "So how is it you can't take the same tolerant view toward yourself?"

Murana didn't say anything for a few seconds. Then, as if she'd caught a sudden chill, she wrapped her long, gangly arms across her chest and around her shoulders. "It ain't quite the same, I'd say."

"Oh, I see. The lapse is fine for me, since I'm only meanin' to be a priest. Different for you, tryin' to be a saint."

It seemed to Murana that Monsignor Shea was being cruel, misunderstanding deliberately. "I ain't tryin' to be anything at all," she said.

"Ah." His expression looked as if he'd just won a spirited game. "You *are* a sinner, then. The worst kind."

Murana stopped dead in her tracks and he saw that she was holding on to herself for dear life now, gripping her own arms so tight that her knuckles had whitened. "Why are you mocking me?"

"Murana." His voice grew kind, soothing. "Child, dear child, I wouldn't mock you. I'm trying to get you to see, is the thing."

"But I don't see."

"Hear, then. Listen to yourself."

"I don't know what I'm sayin' half the time."

"You just told me you haven't tried to be anything at all. Do you hear that? Could a human soul say a sadder thing?"

"But I didn't mean..."

"Of course you didn't. But still, Murana. *Still.* Our Lord's told us often enough He wants us to love Him, to be good to one another. But erase ourselves? I promise you He never intended that. God wants us to *make* something of ourselves."

"I know that, Father. I believe I do. Only I don't know how. Not now. Not here."

Monsignor Shea reached over, took Murana's hands and pulled them from her shoulders. Her fingers were chilled. Pressing her two hands together between his palms, pleading with her, he said, "It has to be now. But it needn't be here. Maybe it would be easier, beginning again, if you went somewhere else."

"And leave..."

It was dreadful to see her face. Watching her, Jeremiah Shea witnessed her first recognition of the full and heartless truth: there wasn't a single thing to hold her here. This safe and simple little town was the only place on earth Murana Bill had ever known. Yet now, with her family gone, her only ties to it were fear and the most tenuous sort of familiarity.

"I'll help you," he said.

She pulled her hands away and covered her eyes. "Oh, please."

Taking her by the shoulders, the priest delicately turned her around and began to walk back toward River Street. She followed him like a docile child. They didn't speak. She needed time, he thought. All she really needed was time.

When they reached the little yellow house, the sun was sinking toward the tree line. The Angelus would have been ringing soon, if only the make-do church had had a bell.

Monsignor Shea sat down heavily on the porch swing.

"Let me get you a cool drink," Murana said.

"Sit down here now and listen to me."

She took her seat so carefully that the swing barely moved.

"You can do anything you like, you know."

She opened her mouth, as if to contradict him, then abruptly closed it again and looked down at her hands.

"What would you *like* to do? Where would you like to go?"

"I ain't fit for much. I'd just like to feel useful, is all."

"And you are very good at that, making yourself useful. You've a strong back and a roomy heart. And all that experience, of course."

"Experience?" Murana smiled sadly. "I've hardly seen or done a thing."

"You've done the work of an angel of mercy for a good many years," Monsignor told her firmly. "There's rare skill in that."

She shrugged.

"And where would you go?"

"I got no idea. Never expected to go anywhere."

"Never mind that now. Pretend it's a dream. What place would you live in a wonderful dream?"

Murana looked at him with startled eyes.

"How could—"

"Never mind, I said."

She was silent. Several minutes went by. Pressing his feet to the floor, Monsignor Shea began to move the swing slowly back and forth. And, knowing that dreams must be born as private things, he looked away from her face.

Finally, Murana sighed like something tight had come loose inside her. The old priest turned, and when he saw the soft, unfocused look that dreaming brings, he smiled.

"Well?"

"Louisville," the girl said. "It's the best place I ever seen, and I can't hardly imagine what I ain't seen yet."

Monsignor laughed. "That wasn't so hard, was it?"

Coming back to herself, Murana looked up and down the street, then toward the front door of the house.

"Don't hardly get me anywhere," she said.

"The dream's the first step," the priest told her. "Why don't you just leave the second one to me, and we'll see after that . . ."

Not two weeks later, Murana had received a kindly letter from a Mrs. Beebe, the matron of an old folks' home in a part of the city called Butchertown. Murana didn't cotton much to the name of the place. But it was part of Louisville, after all, and Mrs. Beebe said she'd be much pleased to have an assistant who came so highly recommended by a right reverend (though she wasn't of the faith herself) through a friend of a friend of hers. She even knew of a nice little apartment right in the same neighborhood as the Home. The salary she offered was good, and the rent was reasonable.

Relying on just a fragment of a dream that didn't even feel like her own yet, Murana wrote back and accepted:

Everything.

No questions asked.

That same week, she had put the FOR SALE sign up in front of the house and called the auctioneer.

Louisville.

She remembered the very first time she'd been there. She was fourteen. Pa'd been picked to go to the State Rotary meeting, because Doc Purchase, who was president that year, couldn't leave his patients high and dry for an entire week.

Even now, Murana could picture the delight on her mother's flushed face when Pa proposed taking the whole family along and staying at the Brown Hotel.

"The cost!" Mama sounded breathless.

But Pa just laughed. "Call it part of the younguns' eddication," he said, teasing Mary Alice about the grand plans she had for their children.

It was smack in the middle of winter, and Murana recollected how most everything in the city—the high buildings, the wide streets, the river—seemed so cold and shiny and dark, like patent leather almost. The wind off the Ohio was raw, but they'd walked all over the city. Pa showed them how the fronts of some of the grim, formal buildings on Broadway were made of cast iron, rapping his heavy class ring on them. No wonder they were so cold. They saw the *Belle of Louisville* idling at the dock, and took a tour of the Armour plant which sent the smell of bacon out to travel on the wind for miles. Lyman had put up such a fuss when he grasped the nature of the enterprise that they'd had to leave in the middle of the tour. Months had passed before the memory faded and he'd started eating pork again.

They had gone to fancy restaurants for dinner every night. One afternoon, while Pa was busy with Rotary meetings, Mama took them through the museum at the university to look at pictures and statues. Then they went to Stewart's, the biggest department store Murana had ever seen. In the toy department, she saw dolls dressed like her favorite storybook characters. Beth from *Little Women* was so dainty and beautiful—just like Murana wished she could look herself. The doll cost a hundred dollars. "Imagine!" Mama said, pushing Murana toward the display of Lionel trains, where Bubba was already raising a ruckus. Mary Alice bought the children new mittens and scarves, before they rushed off to meet Pa, who'd promised to take them in a taxi to see Churchill Downs.

The racetrack was all closed up for the winter; they had to look through a gate. It reminded Murana of the rich folks' houses on the thoroughbred farms near Lexington. It seemed almost sad, though, such an elegant place with nobody there to take pleasure in it. But Pa told how it would be on Derby Day, with thousands of people and the May flowers in bloom and the jockeys in their brilliant silk britches like flowers, too, sitting tall on the finest horses in all America.

Then, Murana remembered, as if the Derby was happening right that minute, her father, with his narrow face pressed up against the fence, began to sing "My Old Kentucky Home." His voice was a battered baritone. Lyman Gene pitched in with his boy's soprano. Finally, even Mama and Murana sang, too.

By the time they finished, Mama's eyes were full of tears. Clive Bill put his arm around her and gave her a little squeeze. "Weep no more, my lady."

Mary Alice cupped his chin in her hand. "Clive Bill, I swear you *love* to see me cry!"

"Long as they're happy tears I do."

The way her parents looked at each other, for a second Murana felt like she and Lyman Gene weren't hardly there. She sidled close to her brother and reached for his red-mittened hand. Then Pa was grabbing her blue one and Mama had hold of Lyman's other red one and...

"The horses are at the starting gate..." Pa cried.

"AND THEY'RE OFF!"

With Lyman Gene in the lead, the four Bills raced hand in hand to the curb and jumped into their waiting taxicab.

That evening, at dinner, Pa gave Mama a golden racehorse for her charm bracelet. And Murana thought that there couldn't be a finer or happier or more thrilling place than Louisville, Kentucky.

"Louisville?!" Glenda McCue said. She shook her head in amazement. "Louisville..."

Riley smiled at Murana, then at his wife. "I guess it ain't like Saw-dee Araby," he said, "but it's a ways from here."

"Girl, this is your *home*," Glenda said.

Murana stood facing her, head lowered, twisting her fingers.

She looked like a briefly rambunctious pupil being called on the carpet by a teacher she idolized.

"Surely it is, but..."

"Who'll be looking out for you?"

"Why, I guess *I* will," Murana said, as if the thought surprised her.

"You'll be alone. All alone."

"I'm alone here."

The second she said it, Murana realized she'd hurt them. These decent people, old friends. Why was it the simple, unvarnished truth should do like that? Lying was wrong and honesty was hurtful, yet folks didn't seem to think much of you if you had nothing to say for yourself at all.

"I didn't mean it," she said. "Not how it come out."

"The Bills has been like kin to us, your mama and daddy and Lyman Gene. But you most of all, honey." Glenda looked at her husband like he should defend her.

"Can we say a thing to change your plans?" Riley asked.

Murana looked down at her hands and said nothing.

Riley McCue patted her shoulder. "In that gentle way you got, you always did know your own mind, Miss Murana. Can we help somehow, seein' it's made up?"

Slowly Murana lifted her head. Beads of perspiration had broken out on her upper lip and brow. When her teeth showed in a huge smile of relief, her whole face seemed to shine.

"Looks like I'll be needin' a place to stay when I come visitin'."

Later, after Murana had gone, leaving her mother's precious collection of carnival glass, Glenda McCue wept for all the things she might have done for the girl, not knowing, still, what they were. Mary Alice had been that way, too—sweet as could be, of course, but she just left a body feeling kind of useless.

"Well, at least she's got a car she can count on," Riley said. "I best run by there and have a look at her tires, though."

The other good-byes weren't so trying. Everyone said they hated to see her go and looked at her a little askance, like they suspected her of harboring a grudge against them. But they wished her well and made her promise to come back often and always. Murana had no trouble agreeing, for her whole known life was here. She simply couldn't imagine it being otherwise, even now that she was about to leave.

But all the arrangements were made. Mr. L. T. Moody and Lawyer Jones would keep on looking after her affairs and managing her income. Her savings—growing from rent checks and government benefits from Lyman Gene, plus what she got for the house and the furniture—all that bounty would stay right here in Mount Vadalia. "My roots ain't going nowhere," she told folks, her heart cramped with premature yearning for the sounds of the little river.

Peggy Anne Sligo cried some and said how she'd always meant to paint a picture of Murana to go with the one of Lyman Gene. Next time she traveled to Louisville for a teachers' convention she'd look her up and make some sketches while they had a nice visit, she promised.

"And Starbuck says tell you don't forget your turn signals."

"I won't."

"We'll all miss you, Murana."

"I'll miss you, too," Murana said shyly.

It wasn't a lie, exactly. No, it wasn't a lie. Only Murana couldn't help thinking how all of them, herself included, didn't quite know *what* they'd be missing. And it seemed downright peculiar, when she studied on it, how she'd lived thirty-one years in such a tiny, familiar place, yet not understanding the people she knew and understanding that they didn't know her at all.

This thought came back to her again and again the last of her days in Mount Vadalia, as she drove around the town in her bright blue car, making her farewells. For the last thing most folks said to her was, "Don't be a stranger, now."

It was almost as if, finally, they knew.

And were asking her, kindly, not to be the very thing she was.

PART II

Lucille

1

*M*id-September was hot and still and muggy as a swamp. Lawns looked brown and scratchy, like burlap. The leaves, lacking the energy to turn color, hung listless from the trees, and Murana felt sweaty just looking at them.

Downtown, new buildings of darkened glass and stone and steel pointed rudely at the sky. What seemed like a million cars crawled over the streets, honking and fuming and moving entirely too fast to suit her. Murana could hardly get her bearings or her breath, let alone have a look around.

She was shocked by the city's grayness, for she recalled it black and glistening. Everything about Louisville seemed faded now. The river was the dull uncertain color of a television screen left on through the blank hours of night. The sky beyond was the same color, only a shade or two lighter. The old buildings along Market and Main might have been fashioned from soot, some of them; they looked as if only the lack of a breeze kept them from crumbling.

But the air, thick and smoky and fat, hadn't changed. It made her think of Lyman Gene, how his face had puckered at the sight of those slaughtered hogs, how much time had to pass before his appetite got back to normal. But eventually he forgot about the butchering, and there was nothing he loved more than the chunks of salt pork in a pot of beans or greens.

Butchertown was a part of the city surrounding the old stockyards. Murana followed the directions Mrs. Beebe had sent her and tried not to mind that cars were passing on both sides of her in a frantic kind of hurry.

It was Saturday afternoon, and in Butchertown the streets were quiet. Murana saw shirtless men washing their cars, cutting grass, watering flower beds. Mostly, the houses were neat as a pin, respectable but not grand. She was glad she didn't have to live right downtown. The towering buildings along the river had looked mean and unfriendly. Butchertown seemed more like home—like Mount Vadalia just outgrew itself and got all crowded together.

Brick houses, painted fresh colors and all gussied up with window boxes and brass door-knockers and little signs bragging about their age—some of them were so tiny they looked more like dollhouses than homes for real people. Murana saw one elegant shop in what surely should have been the fire station. Where would they be keeping the fire trucks now? she wondered. But her uneasiness over the question was swept away entirely when she glanced to the other side of the street:

St. Joseph's Church. It had to be. Murana knew it even before the sign caught her eye. And here she was, not five minutes in Butchertown and right on it like a homing pigeon. It seemed to her like the Lord's message, that this was a place where she'd be able to find her way. . . .

The church was immense, made of rich rose brick. Its twin spires, their tiles flashing silver in the sun, soared high into the sky, like they meant to sweep up the whole huge structure and bear it away to heaven.

Murana parked the car under the shade of a small tree and carefully locked the doors, remembering Mama's Oneida sterling stashed under the front seat. For several moments she stood at the foot of the church steps, gaping, before she realized she was clutching the car keys so tight their jagged edges were cutting painfully into her palm. She slipped the keys into her skirt pocket and continued to stare at the church. She returned slowly to the car, looking back at the church several times, before she finally drove away.

Weeks ago, when Lucille Beebe, LPN (Licensed Practical Nurse—Murana had gone to look it up in the library), had written to her, the Pleasant Knoll Home had formed itself like a picture in Murana's mind: a solid building, perhaps three stories high and made of dark brick the color of dried blood. Its shape would be a perfect, uncompromising square, its windows neatly slashed with bars. A tall iron fence would keep strangers out and trees at a distance. In short, Murana expected a replica of the County Home in Pikeville, a building with no two ways about it.

She'd gone there with her class each year at Christmastime, caroling to those her teachers were apt to call "the needy," though Mama said "the less fortunate" was a nicer way of putting it. Murana remembered stifling stale heat laden with odors: medicine and unwashed hair, Campbell's tomato soup and soiled socks. The County Home was the only part of Christmas Murana had been unable to love with all her heart, but she hadn't confessed so to a soul. There was one older boy with a large head and bulging eyes who was always trying to sing along on "We Wish You a Merry Christmas." Only he couldn't seem to keep up with the younger children. His lips didn't move right and spit would run down his chin. Sometimes on Christmas Day, still thinking of him, Murana would not feel like eating and Mama would ask was she taking sick.

The matron's directions, in a bold script Murana admired, were clear and precise—she found the Home without a lick of trouble. She meant to drive past, only slowing down for a quick look before continuing up the street to her new apartment. But the sight of the Home forced her to pull over once again. She had to get hold of herself.

There wasn't the slightest resemblance between the dreary County Home and Pleasant Knoll. In fact, this place was a *mansion*—no other word for it. Set far back on a sloping lawn, inside a gentle embrace of trees, the building was stacked in white layers like a wedding cake. Long wings fanned out from either side. There was a wide front porch, with fancywork columns to hold the roof over a row of stately wicker chairs. Beside each chair, a little wicker table stood like a stiff doily on legs. At both ends of the porch, lilac-cushioned gliders waited to catch a breeze.

Murana sat in the sweltering car, gripping the steering wheel. She'd never be able to fit in here. A place like the County Home would have dampened her spirits, surely, but at least she'd have belonged there. Pleasant Knoll, however, was another kettle of fish. She'd feel conspicuous and unsightly as a hobo or clown. Then she'd turn anxious and clumsy and start breaking valuable things with her big paws and she'd be fired in no time flat. Even if she bought new white shoes and wore her pearl earrings and went to the hairdresser every week, Murana couldn't see how on earth she was going to get on in such a dignified place.

An old gentleman with a cane slipped out the front door onto the porch. He was wearing a pinkish seersucker suit and a black string tie with a white shirt, and the top of his bald head looked shiny and fragile as a crystal ball in a fortune-teller's parlor. He paused for a moment and seemed to peer suspiciously at Murana's car. Then, with his cane testing out the floorboards in his advance, he continued on toward the glider on the shaded north side of the veranda.

But the glider seemed to want no part of him. It bucked and swayed and slid away. He centered himself in front of it and tried to sneak up on the cushions with his skinny backside, but the glider saw him coming and skittered back. Then it swung forward, hitting behind the knees so that he nearly fell.

The old man turned around and smacked the cushioned seat with his cane. It shimmied and reared. He backed up to it again, sneaky this time, going into a crouch...

Murana watched the old soul's stiff gymnastics with her

heart in her mouth. He was going to wind up on that porch floor, she knew, and a person that age falling . . . well, he'd be lucky if he didn't break a hip. Which would be the end of him for certain.

Framed between two ornate white columns, curled into the shape of a question mark, stiff-kneed and humpbacked, the old man waited for the agitated swing to slow down. His cane slipped from his hand and lay on the floor in front of him.

Murana jumped out of the car, leaving the engine running, and galloped up the front walk. "Hold on there, let me give you a hand!"

The old man seemed frozen in his tortured position. Murana took the three steps to the porch in one leap and grabbed hold of his elbow to steady him while she retrieved his cane. She put it into his hand.

"There, now," she said, still gripping his arm.

The man's gnarled fingers, dappled with liver spots, tightened around the stick, in the middle. Then he swung around and rapped Murana sharply on the shoulder with its hooked end. "Who invited *you?*" he said.

She cried out more in shock than pain, though the whack he'd given her was a sound one. The old gent was stronger than he looked.

"You're trespassing," he said.

"Lord, no. I'm trying to give you a hand."

"What you're trying to do is molest me, and I won't have it."

He raised his cane again, and Murana quickly dropped his elbow and began backing away. "I startled you, I reckon. But I only meant to help."

"Help!" the old man cried. "Help!"

"Now, you see here . . . I surely didn't . . ."

"I'll throw the book at you, so help me God . . . *help!*"

Behind her, Murana heard quick footsteps and the squeak of the opening screen door.

"What in the name of the Sears Roebuck catalog is going

on out here? You all right, Judge?"

The old man grinned. "Assault and battery," he said. "Attempted robbery. Molesting an octogenarian and contempt of court and public lewdness."

"That's all?"

Murana, her cheeks afire with embarrassment, turned and found herself facing the handsomest woman she'd ever seen.

"I was trying to help, is all."

The woman looked at her with eyes as blue as a milk of magnesia bottle. Her hair was lacquered and curled and twisted and pinned into a fantastical complication the color of a coxcomb. Dangling from her ears were gold tassels. Murana noticed they were near as long as the fringe on the old silk piano cover Mama used to wear for a shawl to summer dress-up parties.

The woman wasn't young. She might have been fifty. And she was stoutish. But tall. She wore a red cotton smock with white daisies on it, and a pair of white linen trousers which narrowed at the ankle to point the eye to unimaginably tiny feet in flat red shoes like ballet slippers. Murana wondered how such a substantial lady could possibly be held up by such bitty feet.

The woman was looking at her with an expression which tried to be stern, but her eyes sparkled and the corners of her mouth twitched.

"You best go on in, Judge. Let me handle this. The ladies was just asking for you. They're sitting down to tea in the music room."

"The authorities must be notified," the old man said.

"Yes, indeed. But you oughtn't be here . . . might be photographers from the paper and all."

"But I meant no harm," Murana whispered.

"You'll pay to society, young woman," the old man told her, moving slowly to the door. His face was flushed, revitalized and smug.

"Get along inside now, Judge. I got things in hand."

The cane hooked over one wrist, he shuffled between the two women and flung open the screen. Then he turned back and winked at the older one.

"Homely, ain't she? The criminal mentality takes a terrible toll on the fairer sex." He regarded Murana balefully. "Hussy," he said.

Then he marched through the door and vanished.

"I never meant—"

The woman held up a tiny, carefully manicured hand. "Hush." She smiled, waving her scarlet nails. When they could no longer hear the scuff and tap of the old man's progress, she began to laugh, holding her plump arms in front of her monumental chest and bouncing on her little feet. The golden tassels swayed until they slapped her cheeks. "Ain't he fierce?"

Murana was on the verge of tears. "This is a woeful mistaken situation," she said.

"Never mind, honey. You got no need to tell *me*. Happens all the time here. Bet you laid a hand on him, huh? The judge don't take to strangers, is all."

"He was ready to *fall*."

"Devilish critter like him, probably bounce straight back up again." Still chuckling, the woman held out her hand. "Name's Lucille formerly-Proctor Beebe. Hate to admit it, but it's me runs these monkeyshines." She took in the Home and the grounds with a nonchalant flutter of her dainty jeweled and painted fingers.

"Miz Beebe," Murana whispered. "Oh, no!"

"Formerly Proctor. Only the good Lord saw fit to pay some mind to my prayers, cashing in that mean Elmo Proctor's chips early on. Now I found me a decent job and a decenter man, so there's no need to be mournful, honey. Who are you, just a passing Samaritan got lucky enough to make the judge's acquaintanceship?"

Murana covered her face.

"Don't tell me the old coot catch him a *real* criminal this time? Be a first, I can tell you."

For an instant, Murana entertained a wild notion of giving a false name. Why, she could offer a whole bogus history . . . being a strangner, she could be anything at all. Only Lucille Beebe would learn her true identity soon enough. Meantime, she was waiting, her eyes lively and curious.

"Murana Bill," she said, her voice cracking with misery.

Lucille Beebe let loose a laugh like a one-man band. She hooted and clapped her hands to her round, smooth face and bent forward, the big goddess-body swaying with glee.

"Well, Miss Murana! How *do* you do? And congratulations on your first round of on-the-job trainin'!"

Finally, Murana couldn't help it—she had to laugh, too. But alongside Mrs. Beebe's, her laughter sounded puny and off-key.

"I seen better days," Murana said.

"And if you join this circus, you'll see worse, honey. Believe you me, you'll see plenty worse."

Murana's new apartment turned out to be better than anything she'd imagined. It was in the basement of a comfortable-looking green-shingled house that backed into the side of a bumpy little hill. From the front, where a white picket fence set it off from the sidewalk, the place didn't appear to have a yard. But out back, around the private entrance to Murana's apartment, there was room for five small trees, a vegetable patch, and a child's swing-set. The branches of one of the trees sagged with small green pears that looked too hard to eat, but the garden was still rife with beefsteak tomatoes.

"You just help yourself," her new landlady, Mrs. Gloria Cullen, told her. "We can't eat 'em fast enough, and I do hate to see waste."

"You think of making spaghetti sauce?" Murana asked.

"Gallons. I put some in your cupboard for you. And pickled beans. There's zucchini bread in your refrigerator, too. We're mighty pleased to have you."

"Right pleased to be here," Murana said bravely.

"Your things is all there, came yesterday gettin' on to suppertime." Mrs. Cullen twisted the key in the lock, punctuating the sentence with a thrust of her hip against the apartment door. She groped on the wall and found a light switch.

It was damp and cool, shadowy and safe. The walls were paneled in knotty pine. The kitchenette in the corner was set off from the sitting room by a bar with four stools...

It was a rumpus room.

"You like it all right?"

"It feels downright familiar already," Murana said. "Like something from a dream."

"Home sweet home," the landlady said.

And there, Murana thought, she hit the nail on the head.

The following week, at seven-thirty on Monday morning, as the night's rainfall steamed dry on the streets, Murana passed through the fancy gate and up the sloping walk to the Pleasant Knoll Home to report for her first day of work.

She wore brand-new orthopedic shoes, bluish-white like skimmed milk, and a gray cotton shirtdress. When she stared down at her feet, they looked enormous to her. Seeking reassurance, she fingered her earlobes, tracing the small clusters of genuine pearls. Then she patted the back of her hair, still stiff with the spray applied at the beauty shop Saturday afternoon. The past two nights she'd slept in a shower cap to keep her hair from getting mussed. In spite of the holes she poked in it, the cap had made her perspire and her scalp itched. In fact, she itched all over. She hoped she wasn't going to break out in a nervous rash.

She knocked timidly on the huge front door. There was no

bell. After a few minutes, when nobody came, she let herself in.

The deep entrance hall was arranged almost like a sitting room. A wine-colored Turkish rug covered the central portion of the parquet floor, with delicate little straight-backed gilt chairs in clusters here and there. A brass umbrella stand full of walking sticks stood beside the door.

A red-carpeted stairway swept upward, but it was blocked off with a scarlet velvet rope. An ugly modern elevator gaped open next to it, a humming sound coming from inside. Murana stared at the contraption. As if to rebuke her, its stainless-steel doors slid shut.

"Well, here you are." Lucille Beebe emerged from a shady green corridor on the left. "Good morning."

"I knocked," Murana said.

The older woman laughed. "We don't stand on no ceremony here, honey. Just step right on in."

"Am I late?"

"Well, now, depends on when I told you to come, which I don't recollect. Let's say you're right on time. Come on. First things first. Gotta get us some coffee."

Murana followed her back down the same corridor toward mingled breakfast smells: sausage and maple syrup and baking powder biscuits, Murana guessed, reminding herself that at least she knew her way around a kitchen. She wondered if she was supposed to bring her own lunch.

"The old folks'll be about finished up by now ... early risers, most of 'em. Hope Mattie saved us a bite. Ain't you in for a real experience now, meeting our Mattie!" Lucille Beebe chuckled, and Murana offered a skimpy smile to her back, as if following instructions she didn't understand.

She was led through a maze of formal-looking rooms she was too nervous to take in, then down a short passage to a swinging door with a little window in it. Lucille barged through and Murana nearly got caught in the violent sweep behind her.

"Mattie, honey, this here is my new right hand, though I'd say she don't quite know it yet."

"Po' soul."

The woman, the size of a half-grown child, turned her back on the huge stove and jumped lightly down from the rubber-treaded footstool she was standing on in order to reach inside a pot with a long-handled wooden spoon.

Her face, dark and ridged with age and slightly shiny, resembled a piece of licorice stick. The whites of her eyes were yellowish, rimmed with pink. She looked Murana over and shook her head sadly, putting her hands on her hips. The spoon dangled against her thigh, leaving a streak of tomato sauce on her white apron.

"You'll come to rue this day, child—*rue* it. Yeah. Might not hurt to start beggin' the Lord Jesus now to show you the exit from this den of iniquity and hooey."

Lucille threw back her head in a rowdy laugh. "Ol' sweetmouth." She nudged Murana in the ribs. "You just gotta love such plain cussedness. Mattie, this here's Bill."

"Murana Bill." Murana extended her hand politely to the old woman, who slapped her palm with the bowl of her spoon.

"We sail light around here, girl. *Light*. Niceties is the first thing overboard. Hear me."

Speechless, Murana looked down at the red stain on her hand, then at Lucille Beebe.

"Behave, you old hellion, or I'll boil you down to one measly portion of bones and wickedness in that witch caldron of yours. Me and Bill's hankerin' for some coffee and a bit of something sweet to go with it and we definitely had all we want of your lip."

Mattie poured coffee while Lucille foraged around the big kitchen for biscuits, sweet butter, and a jar of sorghum. "There by the window, sit," the matron told Murana over her shoulder. "Just making sure this rascal ain't holding out on us . . . she keeps all the best stuff to take home."

Mattie grinned. "Not so much like I used to. So easy foolin' a fool ... why, I near lost my interest in stealing from you, Miz Luce."

She sauntered over to the table by the window, carrying two cups without saucers. Her small round behind swayed exaggeratedly. It was the only part of her body that seemed to have any flesh on it, Murana noticed, and she used it like a limb: pointing, shoving things out of her way, closing cabinet doors.

She set the coffee on the table.

"Thank you kindly." Murana sounded abashed.

"I s'pose you'll be 'spectin' cream and sugar, too?"

"If it's not trouble." Murana wished she dared ask for a napkin to wipe her sticky hand, but she kept it curled in her lap, under the edge of the table.

The old woman started to move away. Then she spun around and swooped, bringing her dark, devilish face close. Murana drew back, alarmed. In fact, she was purely terrified.

The smack of a noisy kiss crackled in her ear like static. She felt warm, moist lips on her temple.

"Lighten up, child," Mattie hissed. "You'll learn to love me. And that's a thing I wouldn't fib about."

Then she pulled a dingy sponge from the pocket of her apron and began to clean off Murana's hand. Her touch was so tender that she might have been treating a wound.

By the end of the first week, Murana had even less idea than she'd started with of what her work was meant to be. But each day she minded less. When she questioned Lucille Beebe, she got laughs and jokes and affectionate squeezes. "Just do like you do. Help me out, is all."

Her orders came from Lucille, different every day, sometimes changing from minute to minute. She worked with her in the office, sorting paper. She changed bed linens. She sat and chatted with the old folks on the porch. She even, one late afternoon, worked alongside Mattie in the kitchen. She did whatever Lucille Beebe asked of her. It wasn't hard at all, but there was no particular pattern that she could make out.

At last, on Friday, as she and Lucille drank strong coffee at the table by the kitchen window, Murana tried to put the question to her boss plainly.

She waited until Mattie disappeared into the pantry out back. "When do I start working . . . for true, I mean? My real job."

"Just what you think you *been* doing?"

"Well, finding my way around . . . just trying to keep all the names straight and take in what-all."

"Well, that's it," Lucille told her. "Your job."

Murana set down her coffee cup and leaned forward. "But I been having . . . fun."

Lucille hooted. "What was you hoping for—torture?"

"It just seems like . . ."

"You're doing beautiful. Now the next thing I want you to do is, stop fretting."

Mattie, sneaking up behind her, wound her sinewy little arms around Murana's neck and whispered, "She got *that* right."

"But shouldn't I be wearing a white uniform like the other nurse's aides do?"

Mattie glanced at Lucille over Murana's head. "She hopeless . . . what I be telling you?"

"Well, she ain't the only one of those we got." Lucille patted Murana's hand. "About that uniform—you ain't no nurse's aide. You're *my* aide. Pink's what you oughta wear. And red, maybe."

"Pink and red uniforms?"

"No uniforms. Just a little color."

"Brighten yourself, girl. That's what she sayin'. Get you some *splash* . . . 'less, of course, you prefer I keep on decoratin' your sorry remains with spaghetti sauce."

Murana smiled uncertainly.

Mattie waved a ladle at her. "Watch yo' step," she said. "Tonight we havin' Hungarian ghoul."

Lucille rolled her eyes. Then she made a sign of the cross over Murana, backward, with her left hand.

Saturday morning, her first day off from work, Murana was washing her hair over the kitchen sink when someone knocked at her door. She threw a towel over her lathered head and ran to answer it, expecting Gloria Cullen, who'd offered to take her to a shopping mall later in the day. But when she got to the door, Lucille Beebe's face was pressed in the little diamond-shaped lookout, grinning.

"Miz Beebe!"

"How do and good mornin'," Lucille said, sailing through the door without waiting to be asked.

Her knit pantsuit, sunflower yellow, filled the entryway like a flood of sunshine.

"Well, ain't this a cozy little hole Miss Mouse got herself!" Her eyes swept the apartment with shameless curiosity. "Could use a little brightening, though. Color. We got to work on that, Bill. You and me'll work on that some."

Murana stood stiff and self-conscious, both hands clutching the towel to her head. "Is something wrong? Was I supposed to be working today?"

Lucille laughed. "Working Saturdays is a criminal offense in my book, honey. I just come by to see how you're getting on."

"Why, that's good of you. I—"

"Go rinse your head, why don't you? Them suds is already marchin' through your eyebrows."

"Can I give you some coffee?"

"Finish with your hair and we'll talk about that."

"I must be a sight."

"Ain't a woman born wouldn't be, caught with her head

under the faucet. Don't worry, though. I won't tell your suitor."

"Beg pardon?"

"The judge—I notice he's gone sweet on you."

Murana laughed. "You surely are a sketch, Miz Beebe."

"Lucille."

"Yes'm."

Lucille's glittering eyes came to rest above the mantel, where Murana had hung the portrait of Lyman Gene.

"Well, I'll be . . . who is that glory of manhood you been keepin' from me and likewise?"

"My brother," Murana said, "who's passed on."

Lucille studied Lyman Gene's face for another minute. Her handsome features were as lively as if he'd been talking to her. Then she shifted her gaze to Murana. "Come on." She clapped her hands together briskly. "'Pears you need takin' in hand."

She led Murana toward the kitchen sink, snatched the towel away, and pushed her head under the faucet. Then her small, elegant hands were massaging Murana's scalp under a spray of warm water.

"Relax. Let your shoulders go loose . . . thataway . . . fine. Now a cool rinse, okay? It's good for the hair . . . makes your scalp all tingly, don't it, see? There now . . ."

She turned off the water, gently squeezed Murana's hair in handfuls, then wrapped it in a fresh towel, tucking the ends under to make a turban.

Murana remained bent over the sink.

"Okay, hon, you're all set."

Murana still didn't move.

From behind, Lucille grasped the bony shoulders and turned her around. "Why, you're crying."

"My mama used to do like that. Just that way."

Lucille slowly picked up the damp, soapy towel from the drainboard and, finding a dry corner, she wiped Murana's eyes.

"Little Mouse, you surely are needing some care," she said.

Murana tried to smile. "I feel mighty foolish."

"Listen here—I mean it now."

Murana lowered her head.

"You listening good, Bill?"

"Yes'm."

"First thing is, I'd like to see more smiling outa you, and that's God's truth. But don't you *ever* smile at me when you ain't feeling up to it. Not ever again, you hear?"

Murana nodded, still looking down.

"And the next thing is—look here." Lucille took Murana's chin in her hand and raised it to look into her eyes. "I got me a lot of faults. Now, most folks figure faults should be got rid of, but I don't cotton to that notion much myself. Truth is, I'm afraid I get rid of my faults, mightn't be much left to me.

"Mr. Beebe, he says the only exercise I get regular is jumping to conclusions. He ain't far wrong. I tend to make my mind up quick. It's just how I am . . . you understand me?"

"No," Murana whispered. "Guess I ain't used to you yet."

"What I'm trying to get you to see is my mind's already made up, Miss Murana Bill. So what's the sense of you worrying do I think you're foolish and such? My heart's set on us being friends. And seein' as I ain't really got no prejudice against fools anyhow, you might as well go ahead and be one when you feel like it."

Murana began to cry again. Her pale face streamed with tears, and her back quivered.

"Looks like you been savin' up some sorrow, honey. You just get on with it. I ain't in no hurry. And when you're finished, we'll see about that coffee, huh?"

"There's zucchini bread," Murana sobbed.

"And all the time in the world," Lucille added. "All the time in the world."

2

Within weeks, and without Murana particularly noticing, the Pleasant Knoll Home came to feel as familiar as Mount Vadalia—like a small town where everybody knew her name and her business, and nobody looked much past that. It was a comfort, knowing the routines and preoccupations and habits of everyone around her. Conversation, too, kept inside safe small-town confines: the weather, one's health, the approach and passing of holidays. The old folks took to her.

Her greatest partisan was Judge Purcell Dudley, who evidently failed or declined to recall their initial meeting. At first, Murana had avoided him. Then, when forced, she approached with caution, asking where he'd prefer to take his afternoon tea. She called him "Sir," speaking up enough that he didn't have to ask her to repeat the question.

"That new one," he told Lucille the next day, "a lovely woman. Natural-born angel of mercy."

"He's apt to be asking for your hand any day now," Lucille teased. "And I'd think on it if I's you. The old dog's not bad looking. Got him some money, too."

"Why, Lucille Beebe, that man's a hundred years old!"

"Ninety-three. But a experienced lover, Bill . . . just what you need."

"You got no shame."

"Thank the Lord for that!"

Lucille Beebe's strong suit was making folks feel independent, seeing to it that they never had to ask outright for what help they needed. Murana had a knack for small attentions, and for listening. The two worked in tandem so naturally and efficiently that they might have been teamed for years. Mattie called them Heckle and Jeckel when she was happy with them, Jekyll and Hyde when her nose was out of joint. Judge Dudley, who had a fondness for the New Testament, likened them to Martha and Mary . . . or to Leopold and Loeb on his cranky days. Murana warmed to the praise and grew more confident. Lucille relished the insults and became more brazen.

Murana passed through the autumn with a genuine sense of wonder—she'd thought coming to Louisville would be the hardest thing she'd ever done, but it was turning out to be the easiest. It disturbed her sometimes that her grief seemed to be blunting. She did miss Lyman Gene sorely, but she couldn't imagine him here. Her memories grew fuzzy. Mount Vadalia seemed distant and strange as China. When she recalled herself living there, it was like somebody else's life, a sad story she read long ago.

After Lucille's first visit to Murana's apartment, they quickly fell into the custom of spending Saturdays together. At first, Murana was skittish, even embarrassed—Lucille Beebe was her boss, after all. She was such a good-hearted woman, Murana figured, she probably just felt obliged to show a newcomer around the city. But oughtn't there be some distance between them? Besides, Murana didn't want to make a nuisance of herself. Surely Lucille Beebe had better things to do with a Saturday than be carting her here and there.

However, when she made a stab at saying as much to the older woman, Lucille just hooted. "Not unless Burt Reynolds comes sniffin' around. And if he does, believe you me, you'll *hear* about it!"

Lucille Beebe was full of ideas. And gumption. Seemed like

she'd have no trouble at all planning out a thousand Saturdays, no two alike. But most all of her schemes were somehow connected to the notion that Murana "needed some color."

Early autumn Saturdays, when the weather was fine, they'd drive out along the river to Harrod's Creek, Goshen, Skylight. Fences and no trespassing signs didn't mean a lick to Lucille. She barged onto private property, shooing aside Murana's timid objections like pesky flies, to find perfect spots where they could stretch out, take a dip, toast their faces in the sun. On Fridays, at work, they'd plan the details of a picnic lunch, who'd bring what. Usually, Lucille badgered Mattie into providing what she was after.

It struck Murana as peculiar, especially considering what a glutton Lucille was for life, how often their excursions included stops at graveyards and memorials. They paid their respects to President Zachary Taylor and General George Rogers Clark and poor Justice Brandeis who was buried under the law school steps at U of L. One day Lucille hauled her all the way out to La Grange in a downpour just to see a monument to some movie director named Griffith.

"Never heard of him," Murana said.

"*Birth of a Nation?!*" Lucille seemed outraged sometimes by what Murana didn't know.

"Reckon my mama musta seen it. She was a real bug on them old movies."

"You ever hear of Mary Pickford?"

"Naw."

"America's Sweetheart?"

"Shirley Temple, you mean? Yeah, I heard of her."

Lucille shook her head in disgust. "I can see I got my work cut out for me," she said.

When afternoon would begin to fade, Lucille started coaxing Murana to come home with her for dinner. For several weeks, bashfulness gave Murana the backbone she needed to decline. But Lucille was adamant, persuasive, and sly. Finally, on a particularly clear and warm afternoon, Murana caved in.

Heading westward, squinting into the setting sun as they approached the city, they were quiet. Then, timidly, Murana tried once more to back out, but Lucille wouldn't have it.

"Roy's been dyin' to meet you. And believe you me, he's nothin' to be afraid of." She smacked her lips like she was getting ready to dig into something tasty.

"I got to change my clothes, at least," Murana pleaded.

"Then I'd have to change mine and poor Roy'd have to change his . . . you want to gum up the works thataway? Just like you are . . . and since I'm the one drivin', don't see as you're going anywhere but like I say anyhow."

Roy Beebe in the flesh was as unlikely a husband for Lucille as Murana could have imagined, a flinty, bald-headed man as spare as his wife was lush. His skin was light brown, almost the color of peanut butter, and his eyes were not much darker. They crinkled at the corners, even when there was no particular expression on his face, as if he were staring into the sun. Murana wondered if maybe living with a woman like Lucille wouldn't give a man that sunstruck look.

The scale and scheme of the living room were clearly Lucille's. It ran long and deep across the full front of the ranch-style house, with picture windows at either side of the centered front door, and just about everything in it was red, white, or blue. At one end a curious fireplace jutted out from the wall. It looked like a rockpile with a huge copper funnel upended over it. An armload of silk cornflowers in a red tole-painted milk can rose from the center of the coffee table, a glass disc laid over a wagon wheel.

Lucille noticed Murana staring at the fireplace. "Gas," she said. "Clean as a nun's diary."

Roy Beebe stood up slowly, colorless and insubstantial as lint against his vivid background.

He took one careful step on the royal blue shag carpeting and pressed Murana's hand. "How do." Then he returned to his red corduroy barrel-chair and the Kentucky All-Action News Team.

"Who won?" Lucille asked, kissing the top of his head.

"Near ever-body but U of L," he said.

As his wife turned to move away, he hooked the cuff of her pink shorts with his thumb and lovingly pinched the abundant flesh of her thigh. His expression didn't change, and his narrow eyes seemed not to have left the TV screen.

Lucille grinned lewdly at Murana, who pretended that she hadn't seen as she studied a collection of souvenir plates in a Victorian whatnot by the kitchen door.

"Roy's a plumbing contractor," Lucille said, as if, explaining this one fact, she meant to reassure Murana, then put an end to the subject of him once and for all.

Roy Beebe nodded, given his due.

Murana began to see why Lucille was always so full of talk by the time she got to work.

In late fall, as the air cooled and the sun lost its strength, Lucille seemed to gain energy. She turned her attention on Murana like a machine gun. Having ruthlessly examined her friend's apartment and the contents of her dresser and closet, the older woman laid down the law.

"There's gonna be some mighty big changes around here, girl," she said. "Time somebody taught you the *Saturday Evening Post* ain't no fashion magazine."

Half-delighted, half-helpless, Murana was dragged to downtown sales, country auctions, suburban shopping centers larger than the whole town of Mount Vadalia. Lucille was showing new worlds to her. Murana was thrifty and slow to decide. Even so, she wound up with a marble-topped end table from an estate sale, a pink cardigan with a shawl collar, and a red wool dress that made her feel like a show-off. When Lucille tried to talk her into a violet winter coat, however, there Murana drew the line.

"You'd be a vision in this," Lucille claimed, buttoning the

collar under Murana's set chin.

"I don't aim to be no vision, Lucille Beebe. I get me no pleasure from bein' gawked at." She pulled away, unfastening the huge, glossy purple buttons as she gravitated toward a rack of gray and brown tweeds.

"Disappear into the landscape like a squirrel, I swear... why, I'd have to send a search party out after you in a coat like that, Bill!"

"Suits me... disappearin', I mean."

"Shit."

"Wish you wouldn't talk thataway, Lucille."

"I wish you wouldn't *dress* thataway. Betty Crocker got more pizazz than you."

Murana looked at her, mystified.

"That ain't meant as a compliment," Lucille said.

In the end, they compromised. Murana took home a navy coat with an electric blue scarf and hat to wear with it.

"A touch of red mighta been nice," Lucille groused.

"A touch of gray mighta been nicer," Murana snapped.

"You got you a regular stubborn streak, Murana Bill."

"It's you brings it out in me."

Lucille grinned. "It's in my job description," she said.

When it came to Murana's apartment, Lucille was even more determined and direct. She decided what was needed and then simply gave it to Murana as a gift. From the cellar and garage and spare room of her own home she produced knickknacks and shelves to put them on, framed prints of jungle birds and flowers, candlesticks, ornate occasional tables with tray tops, and a set of orange tin canisters shaped like a row of buildings. Because all these things were presents, Murana saw no choice but to be gracious, say thank you, and live with them.

It seemed like just about the only thing she had that Lucille really approved of was the Hosanna Quilt.

The first time she saw it, Lucille halted at the door to her friend's bedroom like she'd been struck by lightning. "Glory be!" she said.

"You like it?"

"Where on earth did you ever find such a treasure?"

"My mama made it. And, Luce?"

Lucille, transfixed, walked to the bed and began to run her fingers over the quilt, tracing the shapes within shapes like she couldn't believe her eyes. She shook her head. "Yeah?"

"Everything in there, all that cloth, I mean, it all come from ...like look here. This was a dress I had for my birthday party when I was five, I think it was. Them bits of silk with stripes and dots? Those was neckties of my pa's. And the bitty green squares in some of the corners, like here? Those come from this most regal evenin' bag of my mama's. See how the little gold beads is still on there?"

"I swear, I never saw the like."

"And she made it, Mama did, from next to nothin'. Just scraps and leftovers, things most folks'd throw away without a second thought."

"She musta been quite the gal, your mama," Lucille said softly.

"Reckon yours was, too."

"I wouldn't know." Lucille abruptly turned away.

Murana touched her arm. "She passed on?"

"Wouldn't know that, either. Some mamas'll throw out anything. Even their babies."

Murana had no idea what to say. Lucille was studying the picture of Clive and Mary Alice on the bedside stand. Her blue eyes looked cold and treacherous as ice.

"You want some coffee?" Murana asked, dismayed.

Lucille's generous mouth flattened out in a hard thin line. "You're priceless, Bill, you know that?"

But then she slung her arm around Murana's shoulders and, laughing at a joke all her own, led her to the other room. As they passed through the bedroom door, she slammed it shut with her heel.

Lucille never mentioned her mother nor anything of her childhood ever again, and Murana didn't ask. But after that, whenever she was visiting, Lucille always found some excuse to go in and gaze at the quilt. She said it lifted her heart, just looking at it. For some reason, though, she couldn't keep its name straight. She called it the Hallelujah Comforter. Murana was deeply pleased, though, that her friend shared her awe for the quilt.

They were not in accord, however, over the sofa—what Murana persisted in referring to as "the parlor settee."

"Nobody has *settees* no more," Lucille complained. "Parlors, neither, for that matter."

"The divan, then," Murana replied, meaning to placate her.

"Divan—hah! What you got yourself, girl, is a miserable old near-black hunchback of a couch that looks like it come outa a funeral home and feels like it means to drum up business for one."

"Now, look here, Lucille, this settee's my mama's. It happens to be wine color. And I mean to keep it, with or without your say-so."

"Honey, it's old as the hills, only not near so comfortable."

"Then you can just plunk yourself in this here chair."

"Well, I guess you got a right to live with misery if you want. What about reupholstering, though? Make it almost like new..."

"I wanted new, I'd buy me a *new* one," Murana said. "I want it like it is."

"Crushed velvet, a true red—now that might be right elegant."

"Might be like somethin' in a bawdy house."

"Murana Bill, how'd you know about bawdy houses?"

"My brother told me," Murana said absently.

Lucille hooted.

"He told me what they *was*, I meant. Lyman Gene wouldn't never..."

"Least he wouldn't tell you he had," Lucille said.

Murana wasn't smiling.

"I was just teasing, Bill."

Instinctively, both women glanced at the portrait above the false fireplace, cut-glass candlesticks on either side of it. From behind a little basket of plastic roses, Lyman Gene seemed to look down at them with the made-up mind of heroes and madmen.

"Sorry," Lucille muttered. "Reckon I got carried away."

"I know you didn't mean nothin'."

"You never really has told me about that fine-looking boy."

"Lyman Gene? He's gone."

"A body'd hardly know it, seein' how you look at him sometimes."

Murana sighed. "I wish you knew him."

"That right?" Lucille looked at her friend closely. "I thought maybe you preferred keepin' him all to yourself."

Murana sat down on the sofa and ran her palm against the rough grain of the horsehair seat. She was looking at the floor.

"How long's he been gone?"

"Not long at all. But in a way, you might say he's been gone since... well, a mighty long time."

"Don't guess I'm supposed to know what that means?"

Murana shook her head.

"Well, I'd like to hear about it someday, honey. When your own mind gets straightened out about it."

"Won't be anytime soon, I don't think."

"Ain't no hurry." Then she smiled. "That couch can't wait, though."

"Lucille Beebe, you lay so much as a finger on my mama's settee..."

"Shit."

A few weeks later, on a Saturday afternoon, Lucille arrived at Murana's with an afghan and two crewel-work pillows. The afghan was made of granny squares in pink, white, gray, with a red border. One pillow had a design of pink tulips in a basket, the second a basket of black-and-white kittens.

"You made these with your own hands?" Murana asked.

"Indeed I did."

Murana draped the afghan along the humped back of the settee and placed the pillows at either end.

"Not bad," Lucille said grudgingly.

"Lovely."

"Now, let's us talk about curtains, Bill. I saw this sateen down in Value City..."

"You don't give up!"

"It's one of my best qualities."

When she first saw the inside of it, St. Joseph's Church in Butchertown reminded Murana of Lucille, with everything on so grand a scale and in vivid color. The church interior was overwhelming, but warm too, the kind of grandeur that pulls a body in rather than shutting them out.

The walls and the high vaulted ceilings were awash in rich pale gold and rose. Statues, big as life, were in every line of vision, every hidden nook. Why, even the side altars were a hundred times fancier than the little church at home. And the stained glass! Murana was almost glad that Peggy Anne wasn't there to see its brilliance. Besides what was over the altar, up and down both sides of the church windows stretched sky-high. Each one showed a different apostle. Philip had deep, dark eyes full of questions. John's face was tender and glowed with the light of love. Saint Peter looked big and brave enough to see after the whole world.

St. Joseph's was run by Franciscan priests, who wore cowled brown robes belted at the waist with knotted lengths of heavy cord. Murana expected they'd probably wear sandals on their feet, too, just like Saint Francis did. But the first time she got a good look at a priest (or brother—she wasn't sure how to tell the difference), she saw that he was wearing bright blue running shoes with red laces. Of course, he was out in the fenced-in schoolyard, talking to some children with a basketball, so maybe he was on his day off. The priests who said Mass—it seemed like there was a different one each week, just like at home—wore regular vestments and plain black shoes with a spit-shine on them.

Murana wrote letters to Peggy Anne and Monsignor Shea and the McCues and told them all about St. Joseph's, the way a tourist might rave over Buckingham Palace or the Taj Mahal. She explained how the confessionals were separate wooden houses inside the church, had their own pointed roofs and everything. The fancy carving and knobs and all made them look like great big cuckoo clocks. Each Sunday, the main altar was banked with a whole greenhouse-worth of fresh cut flowers. And in the back, at each side of the center aisle, holy water fonts were held out by angel statues as tall as school-age children at least. One wore a robe of coral, the other aquamarine. Murana described it all in detail, omitting only the stained-glass windows, to spare Peggy Anne's feelings.

In spite of her awe at the church's beauty, though, Murana was disappointed by St. Joseph's in some way she couldn't name. Attending Mass faithfully each week, she dipped her fingers into the golden bowl offered by one of the near-life-size angels and felt sad, remembering the holy water font left behind in the little storefront church. Everything here was so much finer, it made her feel guilty that she couldn't seem to like it half so well. After all, a feed store might be better than nothing, but it surely was no house truly fit for God.

At the Kiss of Peace after the Consecration, when the worshipers murmured to each other and clasped hands, Murana searched the faces of those who wished her peace, yearning for some sign of warmth or interest or even curiosity. But "Peace be with you" was rattled off with a kind of detachment.

No one spoke to her on the steps outside. No one smiled in the parking lot across from Bakery Square. Murana took to sitting near the side door so she could slip out as soon as the priest said, "Let us go forth to love and serve the Lord."

It seemed that city people just had different ways, different kinds of lives than she was used to. Even when they looked at you, spoke right to you, it was like they really weren't taking you in. Murana found it worse than being a stranger— this feeling that she might as well have been downright invisible. Many of the people who went to St. Joseph's were well on in years, too, and she noticed that the old ladies all held their pocketbooks tight and close, like they expected to be robbed every minute.

Sunday ritual and duty reminded Murana that she was alone, without kin or cunning, in the city and in the world.

But then this awareness also helped her to remember to thank the Lord for sending her a friend.

Lucille was like a bright-hot white light shed on the whole of Murana's new life. Or almost the whole of it. Lucille, who said she'd had church "up to here" with her first husband, saved the Lord's day for Mr. Beebe. So for Murana Sundays were like little corners the light didn't quite reach; they stayed slightly chilly and dim.

From Saturday night until Monday morning, Murana chided herself into gratitude to the rest of the week for being so richly filled by her friend. She washed her hair and baked sweet things to carry to work and have with coffee. She cleaned and tidied her apartment. When the weather was fair, she took walks through Butchertown, memorizing the street names and studying the people she saw, trying to guess whether they were at home here, or visitors, or something in between like herself. When she was lonely, she whispered remarks to Lyman Gene, but they were mostly about her new life and Lucille, and she wondered if her brother could still understand her. It had dawned on her that she was hardly the same person he'd known. She worried that her whispers might annoy him, like the unwelcome chatter of a stranger on a train late at night, speeding through the darkness, trapped together inside a tight little container of light.

The last Monday in October, as Murana and Lucille sat down to their coffee break, Mattie suddenly dragged an extra chair to the table and sat down between them.

"Well, this *is* a honor!" Lucille said.

Mattie glared at her. "We got business, Miz High an' Mighty."

Murana started to get up. "I'll just step out..."

"Hmmph." The old woman signified her contempt for such delicacy.

"Lord a mercy, no!" Lucille cried. "Don't leave me alone with this evil old thing."

"You a witch," Mattie said, pleased. "She a witch."

Murana nodded vaguely, sitting back down.

"That remind you of anything, Miz Luce?"

"I don't need no reminding of your eternal meanness—if that's your drift."

"But maybe you need reminding of other things, seeing as you a fool." Mattie cackled. *"Boo!"*

"Halloween," Lucille groaned, raising her eyes toward the ceiling. "This black she-cat takes it downright personal if we don't make some big to-do over Halloween. It's her national holiday."

"The old folks 'spects it."

"Well, I guess they do. You got anything in mind?"

"I got in mind to quit this job 'fore I be makin' any eight dozen orange cookies with faces again. That pastry tube is the devil's own handiwork."

"How about candy cups, then, like those pink ones we got for Easter only orange?"

"I'll do it," Murana said.

Mattie and Lucille turned to her.

"Let me make the cookies. Better still, cupcakes—that do?"

"That do craziness how *that* do. You think I'll be havin' you mess up my kitchen?"

"I'll make them at home."

"We'll stay late for supper..." Lucille's face was breaking into a grin.

"With costumes?" Murana said.

"Yes, indeed."

"You both a bigger fool than I thought. I got me great-grandchildren with more sense."

"Don't you fret, Mattie." Lucille patted the knotty back of the old woman's hand. "With a face like you got, I wouldn't concern myself with no costume."

On Friday morning, the backseat and trunk of Murana's car were taken up with four foil cookie sheets of tangerine-frosted cupcakes. She'd been up until two o'clock in the morning putting the candy corn eyes and teeth on them.

Beside her, on the front seat, the box from her new winter coat was filled with dress-up paraphernalia from the Goodwill shop downtown. Just thinking about the surprise Lucille had in store made Murana smile as she pulled in and parked in the small lot behind the Home.

The morning was cool and crisp, with gaudy swatches of red and gold still stuck to many of the trees. Murana looked up at the turreted back corner of Pleasant Knoll and studied the sky. It was a deep shade, nearly as clear and startled-looking as Lucille's eyes. She hummed as she gingerly removed the first tray of cakes from the backseat and carried it toward the kitchen door. Didn't hardly feel like no day for monsters and skeletons.

Perhaps because they'd already grown used to sharing every scheme, Lucille and Murana had to steer clear of each other most of the day to keep their secrets safe. When their paths did cross, they taunted each other with mysterious smiles and smirks.

In the kitchen, Mattie grumbled about nonsense and she-nanigans as she prepared the special supper and served a better-than-usual lunch. She said nothing about Murana's cupcakes except they were Satan's nuisance, getting in her way. But when Murana wandered into the kitchen late in the afternoon to get a cup of coffee, she noticed green gum-drop stems had been added to her jack-o'-lantern cakes and fluted paper cups of licorice and orange candies were lined up beside them.

"Why, Mattie, look what you done, you sweet thing!"

She glared at Murana. "*Ain't* sweet. It's slander's what that is."

At six o'clock on the button, one of the teenaged busboys unlatched the curtained glass doors to the dining room and stepped back as the entire population of the Pleasant Knoll Home shuffled and tapped past—the old folks were always punctual and never forgetful when it came to meals.

Orange, black, and yellow crepe paper streamers swooped from the great chandelier to the corners of the long room. Mattie's candy favors and orange paper napkins decorated the tables, along with a pair of candles and a small carved pumpkin in the center of each.

Mrs. Royce and Miss Lightner exclaimed over the candy cups, with some slight and cordial dissent as to whether "cun-ning" or "precious" was just the right word.

Mr. Sidney Charleson wondered whether the pumpkins were edible and hoped the seeds had been saved for toasting.

Judge Dudley delivered a stern opinion, citing precedent, concerning the violation of city fire regulations as pertaining to lighted candles in quasi-public facilities.

Mrs. Royce and Miss Lightner told him to shut up, in accord that "hush" was too weak a word, given the circumstances and sentiments of the occasion.

Mrs. Kinsella remarked that the evening was cool.

At seven minutes past six, when the gentlefolk of Pleasant Knoll were seated according to custom, fidgeting as they waited for supper to appear, a dainty hand reached inside the dining room and dimmed the lights.

One of the ladies, most likely Mrs. Kinsella, cried out in alarm, and an anxious murmuring arose.

An eerie moan drew attention to the doorway: those who didn't hear it with their own ears simply followed the eyes of the others until everyone was looking toward the glass doors.

A rather large and well-padded wraith stepped into the room, attired from neck to toe in gray: shapeless long-sleeved dress, stockings, shoes, even its gloves were the nondescript shade of a snow-heavy sky. The large head was fitted with a cheap, flat wig of lackluster brown that looked more like old shoe-leather than hair. The face was powdered to a sickly pallor. A small pair of wings and a halo, fashioned from coat hangers and cheesecloth, bobbed slightly as the figure glided forth into the room.

"Saints preserve us!" Mrs. Kinsella whispered.

"Why, that's Lucille Beebe!" Judge Dudley cried.

"Will you hush?" Miss Lightner and Mrs. Royce hissed in unison, nearly snuffing out their candles.

Lucille was still gliding around the large candlelit room giving forth groans of anguish and an occasional giggle, when a rawboned hand adorned with scarlet nail polish and many rings reached in from the kitchen doorway. It flipped one switch and the dining room was suddenly ablaze with light.

Many of the old people gasped and drew back in their chairs.

One jeweled finger pointed, and Lucille froze in her tracks.

The kitchen door swung open with a creak. A gaunt, ungainly creature, crude-jointed as a wooden marionette, crossed the threshold, led by a mammoth bosom, unfortunately lopsided.

Its clothing was every brilliant hue and bold pattern imaginable—an advancing battle of stripes and plaids, flowers and spots. Fuchsia stockings sagged around meager ankles, and a variety of gaudy jewelry dangled from all its extremities. Blinding as a western sunset, an elaborate wig of coils and curls slipped to the left as the vision traipsed across the room on golden-spike heels. The concave cheeks and oddly smiling lips were smeared with a cherry-color stain. The lowered eyelids were sapphire, their edges caked with black.

"Why, that's Miss Murana Bill's who that is," the judge said, jutting his chin toward Mrs. Royce and Miss Lightner.

They paid him no mind. Like everyone else, the ladies were mesmerized by the two apparitions about to meet in the middle of the room.

They came to a stop, facing each other, directly below the chandelier. Its glare fell impartially, heightening one's garishness, the other's pallor.

Lucille spoke first, her powdered lips grinning like a death's-head. "Well, if you ain't a vision!" Her voice, unusually soft, escaped the audience.

Murana studied her friend for a moment, a thoughtful expression on her face. "I wish you'd get you some color, Lucille," she said.

When Mattie strode in a moment later, three busboys with bowls of succotash hustling behind her, Lucille and Murana were still the center of attention in the dining room, laughing so hard that tears were streaking their makeup.

They embraced, their colors running onto each other, as the old people watched, speechless, confused, fascinated.

3

*I*t was a severe winter, with more snow than Kentuckians had seen in a generation. Or so folks said in Louisville, where exaggeration, Lucille claimed, was one of the social graces most highly prized.

The treachery of the ice was real enough. Murana was thankful she'd found a place to live where she could walk to work, but even walking was endangerment. Coated with ice, the black iron spikes of the fences and gates looked more than ever like medieval weapons. But a dusting of snow on the roof added to the enchantment of each small house. Butchertown seemed more like a village now. Captivated, Murana would forget to watch her own step. More than once she lost her footing on the slick sidewalks and staggered into Pleasant Knoll with ice chips matted on her coat, runs in her stockings. She bought herself a pair of heavy rubber boots with gridded soles and took to carrying her umbrella like a walking stick, stabbing through the frozen crust and leaning heavily on the prop until her feet seemed inclined to stay put beneath her.

At dawn, as the wind shrieked, battering the small green house until it groaned, Murana would snuggle deeper under the Hosanna Quilt and think back on Christmas. It came to her so automatically her first waking moments that she felt sure she must have been dreaming of it all night—her first Christmas in Louisville.

Christmas: playing it out again each morning helped set Murana's feet on the icy basement floor and got her through the worst of a hard winter.

Lucille had the tree up in the Pleasant Knoll music room by the first week in December, and a sprig of mistletoe hanging above the door to each resident's room, magic or mischief clandestinely conducted during the middle of one night. With Murana limping along behind her, Lucille scouted and pillaged nearly every store in the major metropolitan area, including a good chunk of Indiana.

Holidays, Murana thought, some women just had a regular knack for them, women like Mama and Glenda McCue... and Lucille. It wasn't what they cooked or how they trimmed a tree. Mama'd been an awful cook, if truth be told, and Glenda was no great shakes in that department, either. Lucille's own tree had been a sorry sight—the heavy ornaments all bunched together at the top, tinsel in clumps, and bare patches all around the bottom. But like Mama, Lucille had a genius for gaiety. She took to celebrating like a duck to water.

When Murana had agreed to join the Beebes for Christmas, Lucille insisted she'd come on Christmas Eve and stay the night.

"There's the sweetest little guest room, gets hardly no use at all. You got to stay. Roy says so, too. Otherwise, how can we make you feel at home like we aim to?"

"But I got to go to church," Murana said.

"I'll take you."

"You mean go right along with me?"

"Why not?" Lucille said. "Ain't hardly nothin' I wouldn't do for a friend at Christmastime."

Murana, glowing, looked at her and felt her eyes begin to mist over.

Lucille snorted. "For a *friend*, I said. Don't start rammin' no Baby Jesus down my throat."

"Don't *you* go talkin' blasphemy, Lucille Beebe!"

"I said I'd go to church, didn't I?"

After that, Murana couldn't think of an excuse. She didn't want Lucille to know she'd never stayed overnight with anybody since she was a girl, and very seldom then. Mama'd start in with there's no place like home, besides I miss my girl when she's not here, and after a while staying home just seemed easiest. But now, facing Lucille's determined invitation—almost an order, really—saying yes seemed easiest. Especially after Murana had tried to imagine a Christmas Eve all alone.

Lucille's high spirits swept over her friend's bashfulness and bore it away. She came in first thing in the morning, all sleep-mussed and excited as a child, and sat on the edge of Murana's flouncy pink canopy bed spinning yarns, wilder and wilder, about what the Ghost of Christmas Past would be saying to each of the folks at Pleasant Knoll. Murana was laughing before she even got her eyes open.

They went to ten o'clock Mass and Lucille behaved quite properly, except for maybe singing a bit too loud. She acted up some afterward, though.

"Catholic singin' ain't worth shit," she told Murana. "Beggin' your holy pardon, Sister Mary Murana, but I never heard such namby-pamby stuff in no *Baptist* church."

"So how come you don't go still?" Murana asked.

"Loud or soft, shit's shit."

"You oughtn't talk that way, Lucille! It's Christmas."

"Sorry."

"It ain't nice. *Anytime.*"

"Aw, loosen up, Bill. Ain't no harm."

"No harm in talkin' like a lady, either, I reckon."

Lucille smiled. "Peace be with you," she said.

Later in the day, just like at Pleasant Knoll, they worked side by side, fixing Christmas dinner, arranging packages under the lopsided tree, and Murana felt she really was at home.

Lucille ordered that the presents had to wait until after dinner.

"All that time?" Murana said.

"Lookin' forward's the best part," Lucille told her. "I declare, havin' ants in my pants is the second-best feeling I know." She leered at her husband, who winked.

Lucille's gift to Murana was a red knit blazer with shiny brass buttons.

"I knew you'd never buy it yourself," she said, "but you'll wear it, I guarantee."

Murana put on the jacket then and there and wore it the rest of Christmas Day. She wasn't sure it suited her, but it made her feel brave and dashing, like some of Mama's hand-me-downs. "I love it," she told Lucille, realizing after she said so that it was true.

She gave Lucille a sterling silver bracelet set with scarabs carved in the shapes of turtles and fish and bugs. "It's for luck," she explained.

Lucille put the bracelet on immediately, and Murana never saw her without it ever again.

"Color for you, Bill . . . luck for me. And," she dropped her voice to a whisper, "a new bowling ball for you-know-who. I'd say this is one Christmas we got near everything we need."

Kneeling near the Christmas tree in a tangle of tissue and ribbon and boxes, the two friends embraced. Across the room, Murana saw Roy Beebe in his red chair, watching television and eating fruitcake and penuche fudge. His face was blank and without turmoil. Skinny as he was, something about him called up Bubba so powerfully that she was afraid she might cry. But Lucille was hugging her then, so Murana hugged her back and reached down deep inside herself, to the place where the strong, brave new thing was. She held fast to it. And to Lucille. And the tears passed back where they belonged.

One freezing gray Saturday, Lucille came to Murana's and they spent the afternoon giving each other home permanents.

Waiting for the solution to set, they sat at the kitchen table drinking Diet Dr Pepper and eating the lemon meringue pie Murana had baked early that morning. A kitchen timer ticked noisily on the counter beside the sink. Outside it had started to snow, and the wind rattled the storm windows. The apartment was warm and smelled pleasantly of fresh lemons, along with the sharp skunky odor of the permanents.

"I shouldn't." Grinning, Lucille helped herself to another slice of pie. "I'm getting kinda like that Incredible Shrinking Woman on TV the other night—you see that? Only the opposite."

"Being your friend and all, I reckon it's up to me to say you look fine," Murana said. "Only I don't guess you'd believe me whilst you got them pink rods sticking every which way on your head."

"Naw, I know how I look. I'm lookin' at you, ain't I?"

"Well, *I* wasn't the one raised the subject, Lucille."

"Maybe we could get us jobs as stewardesses on a UFO."

"You could do that. You got such a wonderful sense of adventure. But what would Mr. Roy Beebe and me do on earth without you?"

"Now that's a thing I don't hardly care to think about," Lucille said, laughing.

A drop of permanent solution rolled down Murana's back and she cringed.

"People do leave this earth, though, don't they, Bill?"

Murana studied the pie and picked off a brown peak of meringue. "They do," she said. "They surely do."

"You ever have a friend when you was a kid that you... pricked fingers, you know, and become like blood sisters?"

Murana looked up. "Never did have a friend like that, no."

"How come?"

"Our family...well, we was everything to each other, I guess. And even after Mama and Pa was gone, I had Lyman Gene."

"And you never thought he'd leave this earth."

"You're wrong there, Lucille. I knew plain enough."

"Okay, hon. But there's other kinds of love, you know."

"How much has a heart got room for?"

Lucille waited for a moment, letting Murana's question dwindle away.

"Don't you think it's high time you told me a few things, Bill? Maybe I don't need to know 'em, but I'd say you're needin' to tell 'em."

"I can't, Luce. Just can't."

"I'd cross my heart and hope to die before I'd tell another living soul."

"It ain't that."

"I'd prick my finger and swear in blood."

"I never had a friend as good as you. But how can I tell what I don't rightly know?"

"How'd he die, then? Just that."

"He just died. He went away a soldier, like lots of other boys. He looked so smart in that uniform, and he truly wanted to go, you know? Only when he got back, something was lost."

"Like a leg, you mean, or—"

"No, nothing you could see. Lucille, it was like his heart took sick, and I just couldn't get him well again. I couldn't."

She started to cry.

"Oh, Bill..."

"He had a bad heart. The doctors to the VA said maybe he had romantic fever, something like that as a boy, that weakened him. But it wasn't so. It was a sickness going deeper even than the heart."

"And you took care of him."

"Not the right way. Just how I knew."

"How was that?"

"He was so hungry. I fed him. The doctor said...he told me Lyman Gene would die if I didn't stop. But he was...I never saw a body so hungry." Murana covered her face with her hands. "Like he was starving."

"So you fed him. What's wrong with that?"

"He got sort of . . . big. And he never said one word to me all those years. It was almost like nothing was left to him but hunger. The doctor said—told me straight out—'That heart of his won't bear the weight, Murana.' But I couldn't deny him."

"Doctors don't know everything," Lucille said. "You were right as rain."

Murana uncovered her eyes and looked up, her face craving hope. Lucille was an LPN. Surely she'd know what would have been right.

"I could have saved him maybe?"

"Don't you believe it."

"It just wasn't in me to . . ."

"You couldn't deny him. I know." Lucille patted her hand with a closed-minded certainty, the way she sometimes did with the folks at the Home when they got addled. "And why should you? Ain't no kindness, when a body doesn't want to live."

"It was like the heart just went out of him," Murana said, sounding, still, surprised.

"That's *it*, honey. And you got a life of your own to see to now."

The wind had died down. In the window high above the kitchen sink, big flakes of snow, fat and wet, had started to cluster in the spindly branches of the dogwood. For a moment, the only sounds in the kitchen were the ticking of the timer, winding down, and the muffled voice of Mrs. Cullen, upstairs scolding her children.

"I never been to the Kentucky Derby," Murana said wistfully.

Lucille smiled. "Well, just goes to show you, then."

"How's that?"

"Life, Bill. The life you got ahead."

"What's it like?"

"A circus," Lucille said.

It took a second or two before Murana realized she must have meant the Derby.

"I'll get you there, Mouse. Don't you worry. I'll see to it you get there."

Spring comes early to Louisville and lingers, as if to cure winter's chills and ward off summer's fevers. For months at a time, the river basin, damp and musty as a cellar, seems unfit for human habitation. Molds flourish under lethargic skies. Louisville winters seem suicide-prone, its summers murderous. But a Kentucky springtime makes up for everything.

By April, Murana and Lucille were back on the banks of the Ohio, stripped down to shorts and halters to take the sun's healing. They covered their hair with bandanas, smeared baby oil tinted with iodine on their skin. Each Saturday night, when they soaked and rinsed themselves, less and less of their color went down the drain. Lucille's plump face turned the rich golden color of a well-basted turkey, while Murana took on a deep reddish-copper shade.

Monday mornings, Mattie mocked them. "Folks be sayin' we related—crazy broiled white folks." She poked a finger into Lucille's rounded cheek. "You done."

Murana laughed, and the old woman turned on her. "*You* extra-crispy. Shame they ain't no meat on them bones."

When the rains of March let up, Lucille had called a sudden halt to her campaign to redecorate Murana's apartment.

"You giving me up?" Murana asked.

"Me? Give up? Naw, just takin' me a vacation. Your mule-headedness near worn me out. I'm waiting for my second wind."

Murana smiled. "I can use a rest myself."

"Well, don't get too comfy, girl. We got us plans to make."

"What notion's filling up your head now, Lucille?"

"The first Saturday in May, honey. Time we's getting ready."

"I ain't got a clue what you mean."

"That's true 'bout half the time, ain't it? When are you gonna wise up?"

"When you stop speakin' in riddles, likely."

"I ain't too sure. But the answer to this one's the Derby."

"Oh!" Murana's face was suddenly alight. "You think we might be able to go? Really?"

"That ain't even a question," Lucille said scornfully. "I ain't missed me a Derby in twenty-three years, and I'm too old now to be changin' my ways." She laughed. "Besides, without me, that announcer-man'd be in a terrible fix. I can just hear him—'The horses is at the starting gate and—'"

"They're off!" Murana cried.

"Nossir. 'And where the dickens is Lucille Beebe?' he'd say. 'We surely ain't holding this horserace without her.' Why, all them dressed-up rich folks'd have to sing their 'Old Kentucky Home' and then just climb in their limos and git. A awful sight, Miss Murana Bill. *Awful.* Ain't nothin' uglier on the earth than disappointed rich folks. So what are you gonna wear?"

"My red dress?"

"Too hot. We're talkin' *May*, child."

"Well, I don't know. Reckon I might get me a new one?"

"Smarter than you look, ain't you?"

"And I guess you'll be free sometime to help me pick it out?"

Lucille looked at her thoughtfully. "I reckon not," she said at last.

"What?"

"High time you went out on your own. See if I taught you anything."

"I ain't believing what I'm hearing. Are you put out with me, Lucille?"

"No, indeed. Just figure now I got you on the right track, time you did your own choosing. Besides, I got the food to see to. I leave that to you, we're apt to starve to death right there in front of half a million people."

"I'm a good cook and you know it."

"You are at that. But there's one thing you ain't mastered yet—the right philosophy."

"What's that?"

"A thing worth doin's worth *overdoin'*."

"Somebody got to keep their head around here." Murana smiled. "But I don't know what to *wear*, Luce. Never been to no Derby."

"It's simple," Lucille told her. "Something nice and not gray. You get my meaning?"

"But—"

"And don't buy nothing on sale this time, you hear? Just in case we got to return it."

"I swear, Lucille Beebe, you're as unpredictable as a county election! What you want to do me this way for?"

"For your own good, honey."

"Never did hear that expression without some harm coming of it," Murana grumbled. "Now, what am I gonna get?"

"Surprise me. But keep the receipt."

It would be the most beautiful day for the Derby ever. The weatherman promised so all week. The *Farmer's Almanac* predicted it. Those who prayed, prayed for it; those who wished, wished for it; and those who felt lucky bet on it. And for once, all those magic dabblers were right. The day dawned clear and warm, and the birds were so sure of the odds they began singing while it was still dark.

Lucille was to stop and pick up Murana at six-thirty in the morning so they could stake out a good spot in the infield.

All day Friday, Lucille had been tantalizing Murana, whipping up her excitement with hints of what was to come.

"I know you don't drink usually, but mint juleps ain't like drinkin'... shit, that's what the Lord Hisself buys rounds of on His birthday."

"You are a scandal, Lucille!"

"Not havin' a couple juleps at the Derby's a scandal, honey. But I mean to see you do right."

"Tell me what you're wearin'."

"Green... to some extent." Lucille puffed out her gleaming, sunburned cheeks in a smile of pure mischief.

"And you're gonna bowl me over, right. Not put me to sleep with one of your mouse costumes?"

"I wish you'd *look*, at least... tell me if what I got's okay."

"Listen here—I'm seeing to the food, bringing the blanket, driving my own car, and I'll get us a parking space and a patch of grass to sit on if I gotta bust bones to do it. I got Roy's portable transistorized AM/FM radio, a extra-large thermos jug, a parasol for rain or shine or both. Besides which I aim to give you the entire history of the Run for the Roses and a rundown of the Kentucky Social Register, including some little-known facts about the governor and his wife, before lunchtime. Now don't you think you oughta manage to dress yourself?"

"Oh, Lucille Beebe, you are *bad* to me!"

"It's for your own—"

"Good," Murana said, shaking her head. "Oh, me."

She was waiting on the sidewalk, pacing back and forth in front of the house, when Lucille pulled up. Murana stood stock-still at the curb and watched how Lucille examined her through the spotted windshield. Slowly, she began turning, so her friend could study her from every angle.

Murana was wearing a linen suit, navy blue and white. The short fitted jacket was checkered, with white piping around the lapels. The navy skirt, nearly straight, flared slightly at the knee. Her shoulder bag and high-heeled pumps were red patent leather, and she wore a small straw boater, red with a navy grosgrain bow in back. A red silk rose was pinned to her jacket, and she clutched a pair of white gloves in her right hand, their backs embroidered with tiny ladybugs.

There was a grind, wrenching in the morning quiet, as Lucille pulled on the emergency brake and jumped from the car.

"Well, if you ain't a glory!"

"I'm all right? Truly?"

Bracelets and beads jangled in Murana's ear and her hat sailed to the pavement, as Lucille threw her arms around her.

"A vision's what you are. You put me to shame."

They stood looking at each other. Murana noticed how the neon green of Lucille's pantsuit didn't really become her . . . or perhaps it was the competing blotches of magenta in her silk scarf. She looked less vivid than usual in this early light, like her tan had faded while she slept. Her smile was a mite tired.

I'm all wrong, Murana thought.

"Honey, how can I lead such a elegant creature to the in-field? Why, you belong up in them box seats with the Bing-hams and the Browns. You got no business with a old nag like me."

"Too much, ain't it? I did wrong."

"What's this carrying-on? You are perfect."

Lucille swooped to retrieve the hat and set it back on Mur-ana's head. She studied her carefully, then tilted the hat to the left, like she was straightening a painting. She tucked a strand of hair behind Murana's ear before steering her toward the car.

"You sure it ain't too much? Nothin' was on sale. I could still take it all back."

"Take *nothin'* back. Never." Lucille reached across the seat and gently pried the gloves out of Murana's damp hand. "I believe you might leave these in the car, though. You'd only lose them."

Churchill Downs, at seven o'clock in the morning, was already doing a brisk business. The streets were clogged with traffic, the sidewalks riddled with hawkers and makeshift stands.

The racetrack looked almost like a palace, gleaming so white in the new day. All those people with their possessions weighing them down, why they might have been pilgrims entering a holy shrine, Murana thought. Flowers were banked and bunched everywhere.

Lucille bypassed the main entrance by several blocks and found a man selling parking space in his driveway.

She rolled down her window. "How much?"

"Ten bucks."

Lucille snorted. "You're a robber."

"Everybody got to have a profession, ma'am." Grinning, the man held out his palm.

She reached for her purse.

"Luce, let me—"

"Hush up." She handed a ten-dollar bill to the man and pulled in close beside a shabby shotgun house with gritty tan siding. "Fella got hisself a piece of prime real estate *one* day a year, anyhow."

"You ought at least let me pay for the parking."

"For nothin', girl. Not today. This one's on me."

"But you brought the food and all."

"This whole day's a present from me to you, start to finish. You mess with that you'll be hurtin' my feelings something awful."

"Ten dollars," Murana said. The proprietor of the impromptu parking lot wasn't far from them, waving in another customer. "Why, there was another place nearer the racetrack, sign said five. Maybe we should go back there?"

"Yeah, and be trying to get ourselves out till noon tomorrow. Thank you kindly, no. We're going in style, Bill."

"But—"

"Hush, I said. We ain't even there yet and already I heard enough outa you."

Loaded down with food and drink and near half the comforts of home—"I intended bringing the kitchen sink, only Roy Beebe wouldn't yank it out for me"—they walked the several blocks to Churchill Downs. They stood in line at a window. Then Lucille paid some amount of money Murana couldn't see and they were admitted through a turnstile.

Murana looked in every direction, trying to figure out what all these people were doing here at the crack of dawn and whether this was the same gate where she'd stood so long ago with Pa and Mama and Lyman Gene, singing straight into the cold, mean face of a winter dusk.

The place, inside, was bigger than it looked, though it was hard to gauge size with all those people, every imaginable sort, milling around. She couldn't lag behind gawking. Lucille was moving quickly ahead, barging through the crowd with her picnic hamper and radio and parasol. Murana had to scurry to keep up, the yellow plastic thermos banging her knee with a sloshing sound.

"Wait up," she begged several times.

"*Hurry* up!" Lucille forged on, loaded down like a bright green cargo ship.

Then they were outdoors again, the sun like a blinding searchlight in the east and grass so green it almost turned Lucille's trousers pastel. Murana saw boxes and barrels of flowers. Men in work clothes wielding hoses. Feet in shiny leather boots. Everyone seemed to be mulling over little newspapers, even while they walked and talked.

She had to stop her gaping, though, just to watch her own step. The ground changed under her high slender heels like a kaleidoscope: intricate patterns of stone, cement, grass, mud, gravel . . . steps that zigzagged up and ramps that sloped down. All Murana's curiosity and wonder were absorbed by the perils underfoot and the difficulty of keeping hold of what she carried. They were swept down into a cool, dim tunnel that turned the many voices around them into a single echo. By the time they emerged into the sunlight again, Murana felt chilled to the bone.

"Here we are."

Already the infield seemed more than full, but in a while, Lucille said, they'd be lucky to find laps to sit on. "Move your elbows while you can," she advised.

It was like an opulent, well-tended park, with small trees and trimmed hedges and soft lawn. Everything that possibly could had blossomed. Murana was stunned. She'd figured the infield might be something like a parking lot. Across the rich-looking soil of the wide track, though, the grandstands and clubhouse and spires looked just like they did on TV.

"I can't believe I'm here," Murana said. But Lucille didn't hear her.

They spread their blanket over the still-damp grass and lined their things up arouund them to form a little barricade. "Won't hold, but we can try." Lucille beamed at a pair of college boys on two beach towels nearby. "Gorgeous view we got us," she whispered.

"Don't you go shaming me now, Lucille Beebe."

"Nothing wrong with a little honest appreciation of American youth." She grinned at one of the boys, who winked back. "I'm patriotic."

"Lucille . . ."

"Aw, we ain't in church."

"Don't mean we can't behave."

"You got a broom handle up your backside, may's well take it out now, Bill. Gonna be a mighty long day. You want some coffee?"

The morning passed swiftly, the sun growing hotter and

hotter, and more people packing themselves into the infield every minute. Murana couldn't concentrate on any one thing for long. There was so much to see and try to make sense of, so many snippets of conversation tantalizing her ear, so much going on at once. Like a human Hosanna Quilt, almost.

By ten o'clock, Murana had given in to conditions and removed her hat and shoes and jacket. Her white crepe de chine blouse was sticking to her back and the red silk rose was pinned in Lucille's hair.

The dismantling of her smart outfit bothered Murana less than she'd have imagined. The important thing was being here, with Lucille, part of this joyful human press on the grass while over yonder, across the track, the grandstands were filling up.

You couldn't really see the folks over there, of course. But Murana had no trouble imagining in detail distinguished men in pale linen suits, their debutante daughters swishing their silk sleeves as they fanned their flawless faces with little programs like dance cards.

But she wouldn't want to be over there, Murana thought, not for love nor money. She'd rather be right where she was, with Lucille, than anyplace else in the world.

As the hours went by, jam-packed with food and radio blare and Lucille's bawdy talk and hot jostling, Murana forgot herself entirely. A sponge, she soaked up a thousand juices from the day. She laughed until her face hurt, ate until her stomach ached, then she laughed and ate some more.

Lucille couldn't be contained. By noon, she'd already made friends of a dozen strangers, starting with the two college boys who told her they went to Florida State and had hitchhiked all the way from Tallahassee to make sure they'd see one Derby before they died.

"Didn't want to waste no time, I guess!" Lucille hooted.

The smaller and more serious of the two nodded soberly. "Never can tell," he said.

Murana smiled at him tenderly, though Lucille and his friend
were amused by his fatalism. If only Lyman Gene had seen
something like this, she thought, he mightn't have loosened
his grip on life so easily. And maybe that was where she'd
fallen short in seeing to him. He needed someone like Lucille,
who'd have taught his heart to fly by tossing it up in the air
... instead of his solemn old sister who'd figured a warm oven
and a clean house and schoolbooks would provide for his needs.

"Wish *I'd* been a boy," Lucille said. "I'd still be on the road.
Why, I'da seen me a couple oceans, the Rockies, and Ol'
Faithful by now at least."

"You might be in China or Africa right this very minute,"
Murana said.

"Oh, no. Nossir. I'd be right here. Like I told you, they
wouldn't hold this shindig without me."

"I believe it, ma'am," the serious boy said.

His friend, stripping off his T-shirt, leered at Lucille before
pulling it over his head, clearly enjoying her attention.

"Listen to momma, now, honey. Don't go startin' something
you can't finish."

He laughed. "You just might be right. You are a handful."

Lucille reached over and pinched him fondly, just below
the rib cage, where his skin was especially smooth and brown.
"What you say's your name, honey?"

Murana covered her eyes.

"My friend here's the shy type," Lucille said. "But I'm
breaking her in."

Murana was amazed what a minor part of the day the races
themselves were. They could hardly be seen from the over-
crowded infield. Still, the muffled thud of the horses' hooves
on the dampened track made her heart beat a little faster. There
was an awe that infected the crowd. While the thoroughbreds
ran the early races, folks quieted down. Over a loudspeaker

the announcer's voice was frantic and congenial.

"You gonna bet?" Lucille asked before the first race.

"Bet?" Murana repeated, feeling foolish. She'd never given that a thought. "Oh, I don't reckon so. I hardly know a thing about horses."

"Think the rest of these folks do?"

"Wanna borrow a scratch sheet?" asked a man to her left.

"No, thanks. Got me a system all worked out."

The man, his leathery face creasing further with skepticism, turned away.

Lucille waited until she was sure his attention had returned to his companions, then beckoned Murana closer. "Three for Roy, five for Beebe."

Murana stared at her, mystified.

"That's the horses I pick, by their numbers, see? Roy Beebe, three plus five, 'cause that man's the first I ever knew of luck."

Murana smiled, somewhat relieved. Picking the horses that way seemed less like gambling to her, and where she came from, gambling wasn't a thing folks thought too highly of. Lucille's way was more like saying a prayer with a special intention.

"I'm going up to the window pretty soon now to get my tickets. Should I place a bet for you?'

"How much does it cost?"

"Two dollars . . . five . . . a hundred. Whatever you want."

Moving her lips soundlessly, Murana counted on her fingers. Then she took a coin purse from her pocketbook and held out a ten-dollar bill. "Seven and five's my numbers," she said.

"You got you a system?" Lucille sounded pleased and surprised.

"Indeed I do. I got me a system for luck name of Lucille Beebe, seven and five."

Lucille grinned. "Catch on pretty quick, don't you?"

"Guess I know a good bet when I see one," Murana said.

Afterward, Murana would think how Derby Day reminded her of the day her brother was laid in the ground beside Mama and Pa on a gentle roll of earth outside Mount Vadalia. In a way, she hardly remembered the occasion at all. It had, as a whole, no shape for her. But its fine points—small objects, particular words—she saw and heard, felt and remembered, with a clarity that was everlasting.

Derby Day: she recalled the salty shavings of country ham pressed between the crumbly halves of baking powder biscuits, and how the mint juleps—the very first liquor she'd ever tasted—made a cold fire that burned the salt from her tongue and throat. She remembered Lucille's handbag, a white canvas satchel, its sides painted with a Kentucky cardinal, Colonel Sanders, My Old Kentucky Home, and a map of the state. The map was blue, with a little yellow star for Frankfort, a heart for Lexington, and a rose for Louisville.

She recollected the smooth brown limbs of the college boys, the long muscles in their calves and thighs, the silvery down on their bare chests. Although she quickly forgot the name of the horse that won that year—its number neither three nor five nor seven—she recalled each feature on the face of the man beside Lucille who'd offered his little newspaper, the yellow chenille bedspread he sprawled on, the way the lines across his forehead deepened when the time came to pack up and go home.

And, just as on the day her brother was buried her memory was imprinted with the single moment when his casket was lowered into the earth . . . just so, frozen in time, she would never be able to forget or alter the near to bursting in her chest as she stood by Lucille, tightly packed together with all those other hot, damp, happy beings, to sing "My Old Kentucky Home."

That moment was surely the most of happiness Murana had

ever known, but the joy was so intense it felt more like grief than any sort of pleasure. Her heart got all swollen with it, until she almost cried out in pain. She sensed that her life would never be the same again, never quite as simple and sure, and the weight of this change, just like Lyman Gene's death, nearly crushed her.

Lucille must have felt something like that, too, as the day ended. Murana noticed that her friend looked peaked despite her sunburned nose and brow, and there were dark pouches under her eyes.

"Best stay put for a while, catch our breath while this crowd thins out."

Murana nodded. "You feel all right?"

"Me? Just heartburn's all."

Lucille leaned back a little, as if she yearned to lie down, and Murana moved closer so her shoulder supported Lucille's back.

"I hated seein' them two lovely boys slip through my fingers." She let her weight go slack, and Murana had to dig the heel of her hand into the dusty grass to keep the two of them from toppling over.

"So much of joy," Murana said. "It takes a toll on a body."

"You don't lie." Lucille wiped her face with the back of her hand. "It's like loving . . . when you can't get enough, sometimes you got to settle for too much."

The infield was clearing out rapidly now, with only a few people lingering, like Murana and Lucille, so the crowd could scatter up ahead.

"Why don't you just stretch out there for a few minutes, Luce? I'll wake you if you fall asleep."

"Naw . . ."

"Here, now, just slide down and rest your head in my lap."

"You think I'm getting old?" Lucille smiled.

"Old? With the spirit you got?"

"I feel as old as the hills."

"You're tuckered out, is all. Just rest yourself a second. We got no place to go."

"Lots of places to go, Bill." Lucille's back slid from Murana's shoulder until she was lying on her side on the blanket. Her two hands, clasped together, were tucked under her cheek. The crushed silk rose covered her ear.

Murana reached for the checkered jacket of her suit, and without a thought for its care, she wadded it into a cushion.

"Old as the hills," Lucille murmured.

She slept for nearly an hour, as the air cooled with evening and Churchill Downs grew still. Over in the grandstand, men not much bigger than ants moved about with brooms and pointed sticks, bags and barrels, cleaning up. Here in the infield, torn tickets that had brought no luck littered the ground like confetti.

The sun sagged until it touched the ground, and Murana sat watch, not trying to put a name to all she felt.

It was dark by the time Lucille pulled up in front of Murana's apartment. The two friends had been mostly silent going home, but it was a comforting silence, filled with words that needed no saying.

Lucille parked under a streetlamp and turned off the ignition. "Safe and sound," she said.

"I hate to see it end, Lucille."

"Was it like you thought?"

"It was like you said, a circus. Only better."

Murana glanced down to the car seat between them and studied Lucille's bag, lying there with the cardinal side up. The crimson bird was perched on a leafy branch, with little rhinestone dewdrops winking here and there.

"I can't imagine the right words for thanking you."

"I'd just as soon you didn't bother."

"I surely won't ever forget it."

"That's what I had in mind, Bill."

Lucille picked up the white bag, unzipped the top, and turned it upside down. Paraphernalia tumbled onto the car seat: half a dozen lipsticks, a compact, a packet of tissues, loose sticks of chewing gum, wallet and checkbook, sunglasses, a racing form, scraps of paper and tickets and hairpins and keys and combs, a plastic rain hat, a jumble of pencils and pens. Even a tiny hourglass, whatever for Murana couldn't guess.

"Lucille Beebe, what on earth are you looking for?"

"Not a thing." Lucille gave the bag a good shake. Some postage stamps fluttered out. Then she handed it to Murana. "You take this. Remembrance of the day."

"Lucille! Indeed I won't."

"I want you to. I saw you lookin' at it all day, Bill. Got it at a craft fair up to Covington, maybe ten years ago. Never did use it but once a year. You use it now. Remind you of your very first Derby."

"Why, I can't take this."

"It'd please me mightily if you would."

Murana looked at Lucille's face, shadowed in the streetlamp's weak light. Her features were animated, as if she were launching an argument, vital and long in coming.

Murana reached out slowly, with both hands, and took the bag. "Thank you kindly."

"You're entirely welcome," Lucille said, her expression composed.

*F*amiliarity breeds contempt."
Mama used to tell her and Lyman Gene that all the time. It was one of the sayings she held most dear. Along with "Blood is thicker than water," and "Charity begins at home."

At first, Murana thought Mama was saying "content," so that the proverb never seemed to fit the text of the homily— how it was best to keep a bit of distance between yourself and folks who weren't your own.

Lyman Gene was exhorted most often. As a small boy, he'd always been enslaved by one or another of his classmates, just as in high school he'd always be in thrall to some pretty girl. Bubba was prone to crushes. His sister was more cautious with her heart, more sparing with her loyalties. But she hadn't been exempted. In fourth grade, her then best friend Taffy Sue Torrance got mad once and called Murana "Gopher Face." Mama had offered her sayings like consolation prizes. Friends, she said, could turn quicker than cream in August. Let you down or lay you flat, show you an ugly side you never dreamed of. Only kin had no two ways about them.

"Hold tight to your family and God, baby, you'll never find yourself high and dry."

Murana reckoned that was so. There wasn't much use in

the whole notion of best friends anyhow, when she had Lyman Gene.

Not long after Derby Day, when Lucille started steering clear of her, Murana recalled Mama's saying, though. It was the only explanation she could think of, even if she still didn't rightly understand it.

It was getting on toward June, full-fledged summer, though early mornings and evenings were still tolerably cool. The Home was air-conditioned and the heat outside, when Murana left work at five o'clock, was shocking. She was soaked by the time she got home. She'd take a long, cool shower and change into a loose cotton shift. She was grateful, now, that her apartment didn't get much sun, but its dampness recruited an army of insects.

At first, Murana was horrified. She assumed the dark spots that sprinted across her floors and scaled her walls were cockroaches. They infested her cabinets, ate her food and wrapped themselves in her clothes. Her housekeeping must be at fault. She cleaned with a vengeance, attacking with a variety of household sprays and powders. But nothing seemed to help.

Mortified, she went to Mr. Cullen for advice. He soothed her. The bugs, he said, were only silverfish. They thrived in summer's humidity. Everybody had them. Murana tried to stop blaming herself, but each time a critter darted out from under something, she sickened with shame. *Decent* folks didn't live with crawling things. And she hated killing them.

One morning, after one of the wretched bugs scurried out of her water glass while she was brushing her teeth, Murana confessed the problem to Lucille, sure that she'd have some solution.

"I swear, Luce, they scare me half outa my wits."

Lucille gave her a hard look. Murana had to suppose it signified contempt.

"How'd you expect to get through this life if you're gonna be afraid of everything that walks?"

Her sharpness left Murana speechless, the first stage of a smile paralyzed on her face.

Lucille slammed down her coffee mug and abruptly left the kitchen, the swinging door flapping behind her.

"Hoo-whee!" Mattie tossed her head. Then she turned from the stove, came over and sat down. Murana's hands lay flat on the tabletop, palm up. Mattie patted them with soft, brisk slaps, like a toddler playing patty-cake.

"Don't know what's got into that woman these days."

"Expect I wore out her good nature with my ignorance," Murana said.

"Not hardly *your* ignorance we talkin' about, child. That's a subject for another day. Miz Lucille Beebe, now . . . she turnin' into a holy terror, you ask me."

Mattie released Murana's hands and they rose in a hopeless gesture. "Must be I done something to put her out."

"You? Why, she mad at *everybody*. You. Me. The old folks. The State Legislature and the president hisself. That woman just plain pissed."

"It ain't like Lucille . . ."

"That's right," Mattie muttered. "Just what I'm sayin'."

More and more in recent months, Murana had taken on responsibilities of her own. Her help had freed Lucille to do the vast amounts of paperwork she'd previously taken home with her. Now Lucille spent hours in her small peach-colored office at the far end of the south wing, her ornate crown of hair tilted over ledgers and adding machine and the ever-lengthening forms required by the city, county, state, and federal overseers of the public good. Murana could see to most of the little problems that came up, keep an eye on the aides and the old folks, make sure routines ran without a hitch. She never disturbed Lucille in her office unless it was absolutely necessary.

On Friday afternoon, however, she had to track down Lucille before leaving for the weekend. They'd planned to go to a flea market in Indiana the next day, but had never decided on a time and place to meet.

Lucille wasn't in her office. She wasn't in the kitchen, either. Her car was still in its space out back. Mattie hadn't seen her since lunch.

"What you want her for, anyway? You cruisin' for a bruisin'?"

Murana smiled uneasily.

"That woman like a volcano—she spit fire and blow you sky-high for nothin' these days."

Mattie picked up a large tattered shopping bag, the stained sash of a white apron trailing from it, and walked to the back door. Flies were buzzing against the screen. She flung the door open with her seat and went out. Then, turning back, she pressed her nose against the mesh. "Get out while they still time," she hissed. "The Lord willin' to deliver you, child, but you got to *cooperate.*"

A moment later, the sound of crunching gravel kept time to a slow throaty dirge: "All de worl' is dark an' dreary at de ol' folks' home..."

When Murana finally found her, Lucille was sitting on the piano bench in the deserted music room. Her head was bowed over the keys, her hands in her lap. Awash with slanting late afternoon sun, the gold brocade furniture and gilt frames and blue watered silk walls seemed to shimmer. Behind Lucille, framed in the bay window, Murana saw Judge Dudley holding court before a jury of smitten silver-haired ladies out on the patio.

"You know how to play the piano?" Murana asked softly.

Lucille looked up slowly, as if finding her way back from a formidable distance. She raised her tiny hands over the keyboard, and Murana noticed her nail polish was chipped. Her heavy gold rings flashed as she slammed her bent fingers

down on the keys. A crashing bass crescendo seemed to make
the air tremble. Murana realized that Lucille had also struck
the pedals violently with her dainty feet.

"You think I know everything?"

"No." Murana's voice was thin and unsteady against the
piano's echo.

"What do you want?"

Murana disregarded the question. "Not everything. A lot
more than me, though."

"I ain't up to this conversation, girl."

"All right." She tried to smile. "I was just wondering should
I pick you up tomorrow, and what time?"

"Tomorrow?" Lucille glanced toward the window, as if the
old folks were calling out to her.

"New Albany?"

"I don't guess I'll be going. Roy wants...says I do too
much gallivanting these days."

The lie was so flimsy Murana might have laughed aloud,
had things been otherwise.

"You sure?"

"You go. Be good for you." Lucille gave her a hard, bitter
look. "'Less, of course, you're afraid?"

Murana started backing toward the door.

"S'pose a flea market seems mighty fearsome..."

"I ain't afraid of no flea market."

Lucille gave no sign that she heard.

Murana had lied. She was afraid. But she forced herself to
go.

Early next morning, she studied the directions on the little
map she'd cut from the newspaper. The thought of driving
across that monstrous, shuddering bridge above the river made
her squeamish. If only she had somebody to ride along. She
thought about asking her landlady, but then she remembered

the Cullens were having a cookout later in the day—they'd asked her to come. Gloria Cullen surely wouldn't have no time for flea markets with company coming.

"How'd you expect to get through this life if you're gonna be afraid of everything..."

Well, a body couldn't help being afraid, no more than it could help how it looked. But she could show Lucille Beebe anyhow—by doing things even though she *was* afraid. Surely that took more gumption than not being scared in the first place?

Murana drove slowly, especially on the bridge, staying in the right-hand lane. When she got across and saw the sign saying "Welcome to the Hoosier State," she realized it was the first time she'd gone to a different state all by herself. It seemed like a very bold deed.

The flea market, in the parking lot of an abandoned drive-in theater, was huge and hot and crowded. Not much fun at all. But Murana could see how it might have been, had Lucille come along. The streams of loud, brightly dressed people, their arms filled with paraphernalia and food and children— hardly no different than a Derby, Murana thought, if only Luce was here.

There was nothing she especially wanted to buy, but that was just as well. There was so much to see, Murana doubted she'd have been able to find anything in particular in all that profusion. She wandered around, trying to make a list in her head of everything she'd tell Lucille—to prove she'd really been there. It was amazing, the ingenious and peculiar things folks could think up to do. She saw lamps made out of coffee pots and colanders, a sofa made from a bathtub, and a pocket-book made from folded cigarette packs.

At noontime, Murana stopped at a yellow-and-black-striped awning, rounded like the back of a huge bumblebee. Under-neath were stands where people with sweaty faces and spotted clothes were selling food. She studied the offerings carefully.

Nothing there would do a body a bit of good, she thought. Then she imagined Lucille, hooting at such a remark. Calling her "Miss Priss." She bought herself a corn dog on a stick and an orange Nehi and sat down at a greasy picnic table under the tent's stifling, odorous shade. The soda pop was lukewarm, but the corn dog was delicious. Murana nibbled it delicately, holding the stick with two hands.

A young man with hairy forearms and filthy fingernails came and sat down on the other side of the table. Murana looked at him briefly and he smiled at her.

"Manna from heaven," he said.

She nodded primly and glanced away.

"Missin' the best part, though."

She wondered if she oughtn't get up and move off.

"Miss?"

Politeness forced her to look at him again. He was holding out a little fluted paper cup. "Red pepper relish," he said. "Just try a dip of this on the end of her. You'll thank me."

Murana felt cornered. She took the cup without letting her fingers touch his. He watched, grinning, as she tasted the relish. A speck of something caught at the corner of her mouth. She wiped it away quickly, speaking to him while her fingers covered her mouth. "Why, it is," she said. "The best part, I mean."

"What I tell you?"

Murana, swallowing fast, lowered her hand and smiled at him. "You told me I'd thank you, and I do."

The young man, still grinning, leaned over the table. "Don't need a dog, do you?"

Confused, she looked down at the remains of her lunch. Then she heard him laugh.

"Meant a *watchdog*, ma'am. Got some fine part-Doberman pups for sale. Right around the corner there. You in the market?"

"Oh, no." She sounded alarmed. "I wouldn't know what to do with a dog."

"Too bad. Price is right." He looked disappointed.

"I'm sorry," Murana said.

"Aw, well. Can't sell you anything, I can still give you free advice."

"What's that?"

"Skip the fried dough. It ain't worth shit."

Murana blushed furiously. Then, shocking herself, she laughed quite loud.

"Don't take any wooden nickels," the man called as she left the tent. She was still carrying the corn dog. She ate the rest in two large bites, sorry she hadn't thought to dunk it in the relish again before she left.

She walked for a long time, not pausing anywhere. She barely saw the merchandise that surrounded her—piled on tables and trucks and car hoods and blankets on the ground. The midday sun was brutal. There wasn't the faintest stirring of a breeze. She'd have liked to go to the bathroom, but she couldn't bring herself to use one of those awful "johnny-on-the-spot" cubicles she saw here and there, wreathed with flies and terrible smells.

Finally, her attention was captured by a rust-pocked pickup truck, where a short Japanese woman, a tall Black man, and two youngsters the golden color of griddlecakes were selling fans. They were the kind that folded up, accordionlike, made of white rice paper with gaudy flowers painted on them.

A handmade sign propped in the truck's rear window said: "50¢ ea or 3/$1." The numbers had an oddly Oriental look to them. The woman was picking up the fans one at a time to show bits of lace and ribbon trim as she waved them at passersby.

Murana started to drift past the truck, then circled back again. One of the children, a girl about ten, spotted her. "Three for just a dollar?" she said, with a seductive gap-toothed smile. She held out two fans, her little hands, caked with dirt, hovering like dragonflies.

"Well, maybe..." Murana took one of the fans from the

girl, folded it, spread it out again, fluttered it once to shoo a fly from her chin.

"Three for—"

"Fifteen," Murana said. "I'll have fifteen. The nicest ones you got."

There were presently thirteen ladies at Pleasant Knoll. Murana would bring each of them a small surprise with tea on Monday afternoon. And one for Mattie, who'd make fun of it. And one for Lucille.

She handed the girl five dollars.

"I threw in one free. For you," she said, as if correcting Murana's calculations.

Murana felt beaten by the sun. She had a headache, and her stomach was unsettled. She'd had enough. How long would Lucille expect her to stay here anyway, all this heat and no decent facilities?

Murana was nearly at the gate to the parking area when she noticed an old woman in a long gypsy-looking dress and huge sunglasses selling ceramic ware from the back end of a decrepit yellow station wagon. Pyramids of coffee mugs were stacked on the open tailgate, with plates and larger pieces displayed on horse blankets spread over the patchy grass around the car.

Murana was instantly drawn to the mugs, which were either pink or blue and hand-painted with scenes of Louisville.

"Look inside."

"Beg pardon?"

Catching Murana's sleeve with one hand, the woman plucked a mug from the top of the pyramid and held it out. Murana looked inside. Across the bottom, in gold script, it said "Abigail." The outside had a picture of the *Belle of Louisville*.

"Well, ain't that—"

"Make 'em myself," the woman said, offering Murana her card. Her apricot-colored hair, short and flimsy as feathers, stood up from her head like a party hat. "Got me a studio in the West End. Y'all come by."

"Well, thank you kindly," Murana said, as if she'd been invited to dinner.

"You looking for anybody special?"

"No . . . I mean, yes, maybe. You got a Lucille by any chance?"

"Let's us just see."

The woman hiked up her skirt and crawled into the middle seat of the station wagon and poked through some boxes. When she came back out, rear end first, she was holding a pink cup.

Murana didn't even have to look. It was almost like she had a supernatural vision. Not only was Lucille's name in the bottom, but wrapped around the sides was Churchill Downs.

Murana wiped a thin film of dust from the twin spires.

"I'll take it," she said, not thinking to ask the price.

The woman nodded. "Three ninety-five. That you?"

"How's that?"

"You Lucille?"

"No, ma'am. Lucille's my best friend."

"Well, what about one for yourself?"

"Don't reckon you'd have no Murana."

"You got that right, honey." She grinned, displaying small pointed teeth and a tongue stained green by, Murana hoped, some kind of food. A sno-cone, maybe.

Murana was counting out the money when she suddenly looked up at the woman, her head cocked to one side. "Them blue ones . . . those are for men?"

The old woman nodded, her eyes narrowing with new possibility.

"You got Bill?"

"'Just my Bill, an ordinary guy . . .' Indeed I do. You want him?"

Murana laughed. "Indeed I do."

"Looks to me like you're in love but good."

Murana's face turned red. "Naw, just havin' me some fun."

And she realized she was. Why, what was there to be afraid of? Even the bridge wasn't so awful. She could hardly wait to see Luce...to tell her...

"Don't be a stranger now," the woman called after her.

Murana turned around and waved. "I won't," she said. "I surely won't."

She got to work early on Monday. As usual, Lucille's office was unlocked. Murana left the mug on her desk with a Japanese fan spread open beside it.

She and Mattie were having coffee shortly after ten, when Lucille came into the kitchen carrying the gifts.

"You leave these in my office?"

Murana nodded. "Got them in New Albany Saturday." She tried not to sound too boastful.

Lucille gave her a long, slow, serious look. At last, she smiled, but only a little. "Well, I'll be."

"And look here—" Murana tipped her own cup toward Lucille. The gold letters glowed like tarnished copper through the last of her coffee. "They didn't have no Murana, so—"

"Bill," Lucille said softly. "Ain't you cunning..."

She bent down and gently straightened the collar of Murana's pink blouse, which had tucked under in back. Murana thought her smile was the saddest thing she'd ever seen.

"Woulda been more fun with you there, Luce."

"But it wasn't so bad?"

Murana considered carefully before she answered. She knew the truth. She also knew what Lucille wanted to hear. Lucille, just now, was more important.

"No," she said. "Not all that bad."

Mattie left the table like someone growing bored with conversation in a foreign language. Snatching the pink cup from Lucille's hand, she carried it to the stove.

Lucille was still standing by the table. As she gazed into

the yard, her face, in the tactless light of morning, looked wan and lumpy and patched. Almost, Murana thought, like a quilt, poorly made and badly used. Lines of something like hardship were bunched around her mouth, spoiling its generosity.

"Luce?"

"Yeah?" She didn't move her eyes from the window, but Murana could tell without looking that there was nothing out there to see.

"Lately, you ain't seemed . . . like you."

"Oh? How do I seem, then?"

"More like me, I'd say," Murana said softly. "You are missin' your color, Luce."

Lucille finally turned and looked at her. "You're like a little child," she said.

"I'm sorry," Murana mumbled.

"Be glad, Bill."

"I'm not understanding you. Like always."

Lucille shook her head. "Just like a little child. So damn dumb sometimes. Like you got no earthly notion 'bout anything. Then you'll turn around and startle a body out of her wits, sayin' the smartest things."

"I know next to nothin'."

"True enough. But you are bright, Bill. Bright as a beacon."

Lucille pulled out a chair and sat down beside Murana at the table. Her smile was still melancholy. It seemed as if she might have more to say, so Murana kept still, waiting. But when Lucille opened her mouth again, she started to sing:

"This little light o' mine, I'm gonna make it shine . . ." Her voice was papery, dry, but somehow very sweet.

Mattie came back to the table and began to harmonize in a rough contralto.

"This little light o' mine, I'm gonna make it . . ."

Murana never had been able to carry a tune. Lyman Gene had such a beautiful voice, though. Like an angel. She was accustomed to listening.

Mattie and Lucille leaned their heads together. "... shine ... shine ... *shine!*"

Murana rose to her feet, clapping.

Mattie bowed, then curtsied, and wound up with a little soft-shoe finish.

Lucille squinted into the stream of dusty sunlight that angled through the window like a slide from Heaven. The sadness had not quite vanished from her face, but the tight lines around her mouth had eased.

Although Murana never understood the nature of the wound, she assumed those moments were a healing. So she was disappointed later when Lucille silently returned to her office, carrying her lunch on a tray.

At four o'clock Murana served tea on the patio, with the fans rolled up in the ladies' damask napkins. Then she went hurriedly inside, not wanting to answer questions about where the small gifts had come from.

A while later, passing through the music room, she glanced out the bay window to the patio. The ladies of Pleasant Knoll were grouped under the big chestnut tree out back. Each was suspended motionless in a formal or dramatic pose, a colorful fan spread against a rouged and withered cheek or the sleeve of a pastel dress. Coy smiles were being dispensed like bribes toward the eye of Judge Dudley's ancient camera, which stood on a frail tripod. Behind it, the judge's face was hidden under a dusty-looking black cloth.

The ladies began taking individual turns. Each tried to outdo those before her in coquettishness. Mrs. Royce, who took pride in being spry for eighty, reclined stiffly on the lawn. Miss Lightner posed in an ornate iron chair, a leghorn hat dipping seductively over one eye. Mrs. Cornelius, her white hair released from its usual topknot, twirled around the birdbath. And everywhere across the grass, little paper fans fluttered like the gay wings of tropical birds.

The air inside was frigid and dry. Murana moved off to

the side of the window, behind the drape, where she wouldn't be spotted. She watched the old ladies, her forehead pressed against the hot glass. Their silly gladness pleased her, but she couldn't feel it at all. Not in a sharing way. The laughter and finery and bright color on the other side of the window might as well have been removed by miles, by centuries, so firmly did it exclude her. And Murana knew that were she to go out and join the play, it would end with the hush that falls over a family celebration when a stranger enters, uninvited.

She looked down at her hands and they were fists, her large reddened knuckles turned white. She imagined those inept hands turning suddenly ferocious... having their vengeance ... shards of shattered glass flying out over the lawn like shooting stars. She heard the shrieks of the old ladies, the thunderous condemnations of the judge, naming her...

Slowly, her hands relaxed and fell to her sides. Murana felt very foolish. But also horrified. How could she even dream such a thing?

No harm done, she told herself. But the phrase was not convincing.

Without looking outside again, she left the music room, gathered up her belongings, and headed home. It was early yet. But Lucille would never miss her.

"Where *she* this mornin'?" Mattie asked the next day. "Thought we had us a truce."

"Lucille? I guess she got work to catch up on."

"Catch up from what? Ain't *been* no place."

Murana poured her coffee and said nothing.

She was desolate. It seemed clear that nothing she could say or do would heal the mysterious injury inflicted on friendship. When they discussed necessary business, Lucille barely looked at her, reminding Murana of that long-ago time when

Lyman Gene had averted his eyes, retreating to a dark place where she couldn't follow him.

Then, however, she'd at least known what she'd done to drive off his love. But this breach with Lucille she didn't understand at all. She only knew a sense of loss seemed bent on suffocating her heart . . . just when it was beginning to catch its breath.

Grief stayed with her all day, a hard little knot of pain that settled behind her eyes, making them shy of light. In her sorrow, she was even gentler than usual. She took longer listening to the usual terms of Mrs. Borden's many afflictions, massaged Miss Turley's neck and shoulders with rosewater when she complained of the heat. When Judge Dudley passed her in the hall and remarked that she looked tired, Murana absently caressed his bristly cheek, leaving him looking after her, quite taken aback, though not altogether displeased.

Her suffering astonished her. Its weight seemed unbearable, and its dimensions left no room for other sensations. Why, she didn't recall feeling this way even when Lyman Gene died: then, at least she'd been able to see the loss as inevitable. There had been a kind of solace in that.

Although she'd continued to attend Mass on Sundays without fail, it had been a long time since Murana thought of church in terms of comforting. But considering where ease might come from with Lucille gone from her life, church was all she could think of.

Sometime late in the day, however, Murana's sadness outgrew itself and burst again into rage. Why, Lucille Beebe had no call to treat her this way. Murana might be ignorant and timid and homely, and if Lucille got tired of her, a body could understand that. But there was no excuse for downright meanness. Contempt. I just don't deserve it, she thought. Surely I don't.

She made up her mind, while taking the weekly inventory of bathroom supplies, that she'd march right into Lucille's office and have it out with her, once and for all. No use thinking about church, anyhow—God's house was no place for visiting in a spiteful mood.

"I ain't afraid," Murana muttered, as she rounded the corner near Lucille's office. "I just ain't."

"K E E P O U T."

The crooked block letters were printed in purple Magic Marker on a paper towel; it dangled from a ragged piece of masking tape on the closed door.

"Best keep a distance," Mama'd said, "lest folks walk all over you . . . turn quicker than cream . . ."

Lucille's door shut—Murana had never seen such a thing, and she knew there was nothing general or accidental about it. That closed door was purposeful: it might as well have had her name on it.

She didn't even pause to knock.

Lucille was slumped over her desk, her large head cradled in her bent arms, resting on the green blotter. She didn't look up, even when the doorknob banged against the wall.

The goosenecked lamp was on, its stern beam directed at the crown of Lucille's head. Her hair needed touching up, Murana noticed. Its condition was downright woeful: the permanent wave gone but for tufts of frizz at the ends, the color dull and purplish. When had Luce's hair got to be so thin?

Keep a distance . . .

"Luce?"

"Leave me be." Her voice was muffled in the crook of her arm.

"Lucille, wake up."

"Ain't asleep." She let go of her elbows, her hands dropping on the desktop, and raised herself. "What is it?"

Murana shut the door. "That's just what I come to ask you."

Lucille shrugged, looking past her.

"Now you see here . . ." Murana's hands rose, beseeching, then lowered again, seeking her apron pockets.

"Leave it be, honey." Her voice was not unkind.

"Not on your life."

Quietly laughing, Lucille closed her eyes like someone infinitely weary.

"Look at me. You best look at me when I'm talking to you, Lucille."

Lucille laughed harder, and harder still, until tears gathered in the corners of her eyes. She tried to speak, but couldn't seem to push the words past her laughter. The sound she made was like a sob.

Murana moved closer to the desk. Lucille pulled a flowered handkerchief from her sleeve and mopped her face, but the tears kept pouring from her eyes, eyes that had turned faded-looking, more like moonstones now than sapphires. She whispered something Murana couldn't make out.

"What's that?"

"You are a caution, I said."

Placing the heels of her hands on the edge of the desk, Murana leaned down. "And you," she said with a tenuous smile, "are a 'nigma."

"What you call me?" Lucille's laughter started all over again.

"Lucille."

"Sorry. Tired." Now she was clearly crying. "I'm so damn tired, Bill."

"I wasn't born yesterday."

"Coulda fooled me."

"Fool is right." Murana leaned closer. "But you best look at me."

On the other side of the closed door, the soft tapping of a cane or walker passed by. Lucille waited until the sound receded. Then she let her handkerchief drop to her lap.

"I'm dying," she said. "Can you beat it?"

Dying.

"Dying?" Murana whispered.

"The secret word."

Murana drew back. She squeezed her eyes shut and tried to think straight in there, in the dark. She struggled to disbelieve. Dying...

Like an echo, her own voice confirmed the rumor.

The dead silence in the stuffy office must be like the toes that tumbled from her stockings, Murana thought: a nightmare she could shake off if she tried.

"God's truth," Lucille said.

Murana seemed to hear herself from afar, speaking out of turn: "Over my dead body."

She opened her eyes.

Lucille was laughing again. Her hand was pressed to her mouth. The scarab bracelet dangled from her wrist, its lucky charms dancing to the rhythm of her silent laughter.

"Nossir," Murana said. "Oh, no, you don't."

5

*T*he worst part, the part Murana couldn't abide, was the willfulness: Lucille *meant* to die.

Two doctors had diagnosed cancer—"the Big C," Lucille said, almost like she was boasting. "In the gut."

She didn't have to die. As if in collusion, both doctors said the same thing: it could be helped. The older and more conservative of the two spoke matter-of-factly of surgery, chemotherapy, radiation; the younger one laid odds.

"We can beat this thing." He squeezed Lucille's shoulder. He had the stubborn look of a rebel.

"You'll come through it," he promised. "We'll win."

"Well, you just have to believe him," Murana said. The corners of her mouth were dry.

"Oh, I *believe* him," Lucille said. "Only I didn't tell you the kicker yet."

"The kicker?"

She saw it up ahead: an old boot, lying in a patch of ragweed at the side of a twisting, shadowed road. Murana held her breath as she felt herself being hurtled toward it, the voice of her death-ridden friend and the peach walls receding at unconscionable speed. Unsafe. Unsafe.

"The odds ain't all that bad . . . providing I got no objection to wearing a shit bag on my belt for the rest of my days."

Embarrassed, Murana looked down.

"Lord knows how to get a body right where it hurts, don't He?"

"Never mind the Lord," Murana said roughly. "You listen to them doctors."

"So I can walk around smelling like a toilet? Thank you kindly, no."

Murana leaned down. "Think dyin's gonna be better?"

"Hope to tell you."

"I won't stand for it."

"Can't hardly stop me," Lucille said. "Can you?"

Murana stared into her eyes. "You just watch."

The broad, soft planes of Lucille's face hardened in a look so cold and cruel that Murana felt death itself had already taken possession.

"Didn't hardly stop your brother Lyman Gene."

Murana scarcely flinched.

"Won't see me makin' the same mistake twice," she said.

Grief, Murana thought sometimes, was like a forest: dark, tangled, endless. Yes, too vast to be taken in by a single soul. Terrors like small animals burrowed and darted through all the places she couldn't see. But work and worry were a swift current that carried her along, not allowing her to pause and examine anything too closely. Moving quickly, looking straight ahead—there was a kind of safety in that, she told herself. Or at least an illusion of safety.

Lucille continued to work throughout the sultry summer weeks. Butchertown became tropical, almost exotic, with fantastic molds and flowers blooming lushly in unexpected corners. Late afternoon showers made outbursts too brief to temper the hothouse air. In the basement apartment, the silverfish thrived and Murana languished.

At Pleasant Knoll, however, the climate was cool and dry

and even. Lucille's face stayed colorless and clammy. Murana wore a cardigan to keep the chill from her thin arms. Sometimes, when the day's heat was at its highest pitch, they'd stand out on the porch to warm themselves briefly in the scorching sun. The streets would be deserted, like a South American village at siesta hour. Across the street, the row of little shotgun houses, shimmering, might have been a mirage. The stench of the stockyards was hellish.

Once again, without discussion or consent, the pattern of their work at the Home was altered. They were rarely apart now in the course of a day. Murana watched Lucille closely. Whatever she did, Murana found some way to help . . . or some other task to keep her nearby. She couldn't bear to let Lucille out of her sight, and the older woman seemed to accept this. They worked like one being with four hands.

And they talked and laughed as much as before. Maybe more. Lucille's irreverence knew no bounds. Often her jokes were bitter. Murana made herself laugh hardest at what hurt and frightened her most, for she believed that was what Lucille needed from her. She swore to herself that she would never, no matter what, cry. Not in front of Lucille. And she didn't.

But that didn't mean she was prepared to sanction Lucille's sinful giving-up. Murana was dead-set against her friend's will, and she meant to talk Lucille into that operation if it was the last thing she did.

Day in and day out, as the summer dragged on, Murana threatened, pleaded, bargained, and demanded. At times, she would be rational and calm. Other times, she raised cain. Lucille was trying to make her an accomplice to death, and Murana was furious. She had no intention of going along.

By August, Murana sensed that Lucille was weakening. She seemed to joke a little less, to listen a little more. Sometimes, when she didn't realize Murana was observing her, she'd stare into space and it looked as if two separate powers were fighting over her face.

But Murana's strongest ally was neither her own determination nor Lucille's uncertainty. It was the pain. With each passing day, Lucille was being more brutally assaulted. Eventually, she'd break down. Be taken alive.

Murana waited, watching the waves of agony that turned her beloved friend wet and white, forcing her to grip the edge of anything at hand. One day she glimpsed Lucille bent double in the linen closet. Murana pretended not to notice, horrified by her own heartlessness. But she was rooting for the pain now. She wanted it to bring Lucille to her knees.

And it would, she felt certain. If only it would hurry, so there'd be enough time...

Murana began to pray. She prayed for the pain to defeat Lucille completely and quickly.

Lucille finally had the operation in September. By that time, the doctors had started upping the odds. The younger one, Dr. Ahmed, spoke of buying time and wore a skittish, beleaguered look when he examined Lucille. His older colleague, who would perform the surgery, was terse and grim.

"There's still a chance," they said.

Lucille didn't believe them for a minute.

Murana didn't either, really. She settled for hope and didn't try to measure it.

Lucille asked her to come and wait at the hospital the day of the surgery. "Roy Beebe's nervous as a flea with all them doctors around. I told him, stay home. Besides, if I don't make it, God knows what he'd pick me out to wear for the funeral. My black lace baby-dolls, most likely..."

Murana forced a small smile. "You offerin' me a day off work, Lucille?"

"Way I plan to holler and carry on, you'll wish you had nothin' worse than them old folks on your hands."

"I'll be right here."

"Wouldn't miss it for the world, right?"

Murana went to the window, opened it, and looked down on the hospital parking lot. It was early evening, and the sky, whitish, hinted at a hundred soft colors. The rows of dark cars below, little spots of light reflecting on them, resembled dominoes. She kept her back to Lucille for several minutes.

"Don't care much for my humor, huh?"

Murana didn't reply.

"You crying, Bill?"

She spun around. "You think that's all I'm good for, don't you?"

Lucille shrank back into her pillows, looking small.

"I'm every bit as tough as you are. You ain't about to see me cry."

"Girl, what's got into you?"

"There's a few things I been savin' to tell you these last weeks, so you can just listen up, Lucille."

The tiny hands, stripped of rings and nail polish, twisted the binding on the blanket.

"I'm just as tough as you and you're . . . you're as tough as *me*, Lucille. Don't you go forgetting that now." Murana's voice broke, but her eyes were dry and fierce. "Not *now*, you hear?"

"Well, all right." Lucille looked chastened. "Don't get so stirred up."

"I ain't finished," Murana snapped. "You remember you told me once how you didn't want to see me do no smilin' I didn't feel like? You recall that time?"

She nodded.

"Well, the same goes for you. Them jokes of yours stretchin' you mighty thin. You got more important business to tend to, so save your breath."

Murana turned around again, wrapping her arms around herself as if she were cold.

Behind her, Lucille reached over and switched off the light. The pink walls turned the nameless color of dusk.

"They shaved me." Lucille's voice sounded insubstantial.

"What difference does it make?"

"More than you might think."

"Then don't you think about it."

"I'm scared. Scared shitless."

"So am I," Murana said. "Only I reckon it's easier for somebody like me who's used to it."

"Bill?"

"What?"

"I want you to come say good-bye in the morning."

"You ain't going to die," Murana whispered.

"Shoot, I know that. But when they get done with me, I'm gonna be ... mighty changed. Partly gone."

"No part that hardly matters."

"It matters," Lucille said. "It matters."

"As well as could be expected."

That was the message the doctors sent up to let Murana know the operation was over. But in the days that followed, it became like a password. The nurses picked it up like myna birds.

"Miz Beebe eat her lunch today?" Murana would ask, passing the nurses' station.

"As well as could be expected."

Even Lucille herself resorted to it after a while.

"How'd you sleep last night?"

"As well as ..."

The phrase kindled hatred in Murana. She'd fallen back on it herself, once she'd come to understand her brother would never speak, would never be the same. Acceptance was what it signified, and Murana made up her mind that this time she'd have none of it.

The morning of the surgery, she came early to the hospital as Lucille had asked, but she refused to say good-bye.

Dazed and drowsy from the shot she'd been given, Lucille still knew how to bamboozle. "Even a murderer's entitled to a last request," she said, gazing reproachfully at Murana.

"This ain't gonna *be* your last, not by a long shot."

"That's just what I got here, a long shot. With everything riding on it. And you'd deny me?"

How many times had it come to that, with Murana never once going against her brother, going against her own peaceable inclinations and eagerness to please? "I just couldn't deny him," she'd kept repeating after Lyman Gene died, until her disavowal had become his epitaph.

"I would," she told Lucille, "for your own good."

Two huge orderlies, bearded young men with bulging, molasses-colored forearms, came to lift Lucille onto a white-swathed rolling table.

Lucille stretched out a hand, as if begging alms. She had thrown such a fit when a nurse had tried to remove her scarab bracelet that a compromise had been reached: her wrist was bound in white surgical tape, the bracelet beneath it. Murana took Lucille's fingers and pressed them to her own cheek.

"All set?" one of the orderlies asked cheerfully. "Time to go bye-bye."

"Say it, Bill."

Murana shook her head, clamping her lips together. Lucille's hand slipped from her grasp as the men began to wheel her away.

Half-running, Murana followed them down the corridor to the open elevator.

"Better wait here, miss."

"*Good-bye,*" Lucille said.

"I'll see you," Murana answered. "See you later, Luce."

Long after the great gray elevator swallowed Lucille, Murana stood in the corridor in front of it, counting the floor tiles, looking at her reflection in the gleaming closed panels, telling herself she'd done right.

But hours later, when they brought Lucille down from Recovery, Murana saw the insensible, diminished face of her friend and understood how mistaken she'd been. Part of Lucille was already gone; she'd come back a stranger, foreign to Murana and the world of those who were healthy and strong and concerned with the details of living. The doctors had spoken of buying time for her, and perhaps by slicing away a chunk of disease, they had. Even so, Murana realized now, a soul had begun its dying. Nothing would change that. And Murana had denied her a simple thing.

Lucille's feet twitched under the covers, and she groaned weakly from deep within an anesthetized dream.

Souls don't die, Murana thought. Not *souls*. But Lucille was dying, and there just didn't seem to be any sense of solace in the distinction.

Murana bent over the bed, her cheek touching the pillow. "Good-bye," she whispered.

6

As hot, indolent autumn drew on, it became obvious that Lucille would never leave the hospital. "As well as could be expected" was circumscribed within smaller and smaller circles of meaning. The doctors, the nurses, and even Murana herself spoke in hushed tones of "making the patient as comfortable as possible."

Visiting the sick: as a child in catechism class, Murana had memorized the corporal works of mercy. She tried to recollect the others now, seeking ways to ease Lucille's suffering. She couldn't remember them all, and the ones she did hardly applied—Lucille wasn't hungry. She didn't need clothes.

One night when the pain was so intense that Lucille thrashed and moaned with it, Murana finally broke down and wept. But she was crying less for her friend's anguish than for her own lack of power against it. "What can I *do* for you?" she begged.

Lucille's arms and legs quieted. "Abide with me," she said. Her eyes were dim, but her smile was radiant.

For a short interval after the surgery, Lucille had been bitter and bawdy. She seemed to blame Murana for her discomfort. The operation had done no good; they both knew it.

"Got it all," Lucille said. "Bought the shit bag and the farm at once. Package deal. I hope you and them doctor friends of yours is satisfied."

"Don't talk like that," Murana pleaded.

"You don't want to face facts, is all."

By October, however, Lucille's rage lapsed, as if she just couldn't carry the extra cargo. The drugs were making her sick and tired, but pain continued to ravage her in spite of them. Her raucous laughter lost its rough texture. She seemed to grow smaller from one day to the next, so that what didn't shrink—her teeth and nose, for instance—began to seem enormous. Her sharp edges wore down, leaving a gentle hulk with only the mildest of resentments.

Murana was temporarily in charge of the Pleasant Knoll Home. Before going into the hospital, Lucille had called the owners, Mr. and Mrs. Haddad, in Florida. She didn't elaborate, but simply said her assistant was perfectly capable of managing while she was laid up. Relieved and reassured about the well-being of their investment, the retired couple approved the suggestion.

Murana was overwhelmed at first, although she didn't let on. The last thing Lucille needed was to be worrying about the Home. "Course I can manage," Murana said. And soon, to her amazement, she learned it was true. She was quite capable of keeping things running smoothly, which was what she'd mostly been doing anyway.

Every day at five o'clock, Murana drove across town to feed Lucille her dinner. Often, at nine, when visiting hours were over, she had to go back to the Home to catch up on the paperwork in Lucille's office. She'd studied bookkeeping in high school, and now she remembered why she'd taken such a shine to it. There was something soothing about the neat columns of figures on the pale green ledger pages, something almost like sport in finally getting the sums to come out right. "Balance" reminded her of "ballet," a magical sort of grace. No matter how long it took to find it, there was comfort in knowing there would be, eventually, a right solution.

Sitting in the peach-colored office late at night, the goose-necked lamp casting a halo of light on her work while the old folks snored and muttered on the floors above, Murana felt very close to Lucille, the real one. Here in the Home she was almost visible, while back there in the hospital bed she seemed sketchy and distant, even when Murana sat right beside her, spooning soft foods into her mouth or holding her cold hand.

The Home and the hospital: it nearly amounted to a new life, *another* new life. Murana tried not to wonder how many more there would have to be. The days absorbed her, in single file, and she was grateful. Even exhaustion was a kind of solace.

Another new life, an honest one, which made plain right from the start that it couldn't last forever, that she mustn't expect it to. Borrowed time. Murana gave herself over to spending it, a cache so infinitely precious and precarious that she bartered the past and the future for it.

At night, as Murana struggled for a few hours' sleep, Butchertown pushed past the curtains. But even when the smoky scent of stockyards and phantom tanneries filled the air, her memory was steeped in the stench of Lucille's room: dirty diapers and vomit and worse things, much worse, as if the very air of loss had been preserved.

Lucille apologized for the odor continually. Murana swore she didn't notice it at all. It wasn't strong; just the slightest suggestion of foulness, like a shadow behind the sharper fragrances of cologne, disinfectant, medicines.

Afterward, however, it was what Murana would remember most keenly—the familiar scent of death, insinuating itself into everything.

The days were growing shorter and shorter. After sundown, a chill crept into the air. One evening Murana carried the Hosanna Quilt to the hospital and laid it across Lucille's bed. "Thought you could use some color," she whispered.

The bed was cranked up almost to sitting position, but

Lucille was apparently dozing. She did not stir, even when Murana pulled the quilt up over her chest and shoulders. As she was turning from the bed, however, Murana saw one blue eye, clear and bright, looking at her.

"My Hallelujah Comforter—knew I'd weasel it away from you sooner or later."

"It's a *loan*," Murana said.

"Yeah? What if I mess on it, throw up or something?"

Murana grinned. "Then you can keep it, I reckon."

"Miss Bill, sounds to me like you fallen sadly under the influence of one Mattie Curlew."

"Mattie? Nossir. It's you knocked the natural sweetness outa me, Lucille. I'm getting just like you."

"Let's not go overboard now," Lucille said.

Then, clutching the Hosanna Quilt up under her chin, she turned on her side and went back to sleep.

With Halloween coming on, the doctors admitted at last that Lucille was dying. A matter of days, they told Murana. Nothing to do but make them as painless as possible.

Murana nodded politely, wondering at their sudden devotion to truth.

"Should I say . . . should I be telling her?" she asked.

"She knows."

Of course. Lucille had known before any of them. Just as she would be the best judge, now, of whether the subject of her death bore talking about.

Nurses glided in and out of the room with fresh linen, rubbing alcohol, talcum powder, syringes full of ease. The ease, like the days themselves, grew briefer, losing strength and momentum. And Lucille, little more now than a chemical concoction, lost strength and momentum, too. She joked with the doctors and nurses when she was awake, but she was awake less and less. She could no longer eat. She reported to Murana that she'd lost eighty-three pounds, pretending it was something to brag about. "This place has it all over Gloria Stevens and them," she said. "Lose much more of this bustline, though, I'm apt to lose me a husband."

Roy Beebe came and sat with her in the afternoons. When Murana arrived, shortly after five, he always left abruptly, nodding at her and patting Lucille's shoulder. He seemed unaware of the look of pure and blessed relief that transformed his face as he passed out the door.

Murana wished she knew him. She felt great pity for him. Men were so bewildered by illness, even doctors. She wondered if it pained Mr. Beebe, Lucille paying him so little mind in her last days. Or if he even knew these were her last days. He seemed stunned, and walked carefully, like a man just beginning to try to figure out what he was up against.

Lucille understood, though. One evening, after he'd gone out, shutting the door behind him, she said, "Poor Roy... don't hardly know what's hit him."

Murana had no idea what to say. Close as she and Lucille were, the marriage had remained a mystery. Roy Beebe was something that was there, to be taken into account when plans were made—but as much might be said for Lucille's Dodge sedan.

"Guess we look like a pretty sorry couple, Roy and me."

Murana sat on the foot of the bed, where Lucille could see her without turning her head.

"Some folks wonder what I seen in him. But plenty of others don't see what he sees in me." She laughed weakly. "The things I could tell 'em!

"Well, I can't hardly blame anybody for missing what don't meet the eye. But there's more to that Roy Beebe..."

"Don't tire yourself out now, Lucille." Murana noticed that she was beginning to look feverish.

"You hear me, honey. This is important. I got to provide for you before I go."

"Lucille—"

"Oh, don't get all persnickety on me. High time somebody told you about them birds and bees."

"I had me a mama, you know."

"No disrespect, but it seems to me she left you a little wanting in that department. Ever had you a boyfriend?"

"No." Murana flushed. "Not really."

"Ain't that a shame, Bill, a lovin' girl like you?"

"You know how it's been, Lyman Gene and all. How's I supposed to have time for boyfriends?"

"Honey, I ain't blaming you for what's done. I'm only sayin'..."

Lucille's eyes dropped closed and little brackets of sorrow enclosed her mouth.

"About you and Mr. Beebe, you was telling me..."

Lucille shook her head. "That man give me such *love*. You got no idea."

Murana took her hand. "Maybe I do, a little," she said.

"Folks look at us, Roy and me, and they say that dumb thing, you know... 'got nothin' in common.' Well, I'm here to tell you, what we got is a uncommon thing."

Lucille opened her eyes again, and their deep blue color seemed to return for a moment.

"I'm loud and he's quiet, it's true. I like to go out and raise hell, while he stays home and watches that color Zenith like it's the dearest thing in all the world. I know how it appears."

"Don't matter how it appears, Luce."

"Damn right. Because every night, no matter what, we wind up on the same side of that big bed."

"Now, Lucille..."

"The worst thing about this dyin's I just ain't ready. Got me so many things I mean to do yet."

"No need to think about that."

"I always figured it'd be a blessing, to know in advance like this. So you could kinda cap things off. But it seemed like soon as I knew I only had a little time, I had no strength at all. I frittered a lot away."

"Ssh..." Murana smoothed her friend's thin hair back from her damp forehead

"I meant to find you one."

"How's that, honey?"

"Meant to find a man like Roy Beebe for you."

Murana smiled. "You think I got stubborn over Mama's settee, how'd you expect I'd take to some man?"

"I picked the right one, wouldn't had to but give you a little shove in the right direction."

"You are a shameful, meddlesome creature."

"Course Roy'll be all alone now..."

Murana drew in a sharp, pained breath.

"Well, you just think about that," Lucille murmured, drifting off toward sleep. "Bear it in mind."

Murana slipped quietly from the foot of the bed and pulled the Hosanna Quilt over Lucille's shriveled arms and shoulders. Her skin was dull and colorless, like waxed paper. The dark rings of pain and exhaustion around her eyes gave her a beaten look. But the brackets of sorrow had vanished. Her lips were slightly parted, and her expression was peaceful.

She murmured something.

Murana leaned over her. "What's that, Luce?"

"...such love..." Lucille said, smiling in her sleep.

The last night of October, Murana was late getting to the hospital. It was after six o'clock when she reached Lucille's room.

The dinner tray was gone...or perhaps they wouldn't be bothering to bring one anymore. Lucille hadn't eaten for several weeks. Her dwindling arm was connected by a long plastic tube to an upside-down bottle. Another tube ran into her nose. The air in the room was a misery.

Murana stuck her head inside, concealing her body behind the door.

"Trick or treat," she said.

Lucille smiled, her eyes vague with pain.

Murana jumped out from behind the door, dressed in purple-and-white jockey's silks.

During her friend's illness, Murana herself had been wasting away. Always spare, despite her outsized bones, she'd been whittled down now to the size and shape of a boy. Her hips were angular, her breasts hardly noticeable beneath the purple-and-white quadrants of the satin jacket.

Gleaming black boots came almost to her knees, and her hair was tucked inside a small visored cap. She carried a riding crop in one hand. An orange shopping bag with a picture of a witch riding a broom across the face of the moon dangled from her other wrist.

Lucille blinked. "Well, if you ain't a caution."

"Trick or treat?" Murana repeated.

"Treat."

Murana peeled off her snug black gloves, set them on the foot of the bed with the crop, and reached into the bag. She arranged a plate of jack-o'-lantern cookies, two apples, a bag of popcorn, and a small jug of cider on Lucille's bed tray.

"Mattie made them cookies, I bet."

"Indeed she did."

"Figures . . . them faces is mean as the devil."

Murana reached into her bag again and handed Lucille a clown mask. "Give you some color," she said.

Carefully holding aside the nose tube, Lucille slipped the elastic under her chin and set the mask on the crown of her head like a hat. The effect of its vivid leer above her own pale, calm features was startling and terrible.

"Two-faced," she said. "That's me."

"Not hardly."

"Tell me something, honey. Where's a girl gonna find herself a jockey the size of you?"

Murana smiled. "The top wasn't no problem. But I had to make the britches myself."

"Don't say."

"Got the rest, boots and all, at a costume renting place on Jefferson."

"Well, you are a treat, I'd say. But what was up your sleeve if I said trick?"

Murana hesitated. "I don't rightly know."

The two women looked at each other. After a minute, Lucille sighed. "Me neither, honey. I just don't know..."

Moving stiffly in the tight satin breeches, Murana sat on the bed and took Lucille's hand. "Can you manage a bite of something?"

"Don't think so." A spasm of pain crossed her face like a thief's shadow. "But you tell that Mattie I ate them cookies, every last one, and I said they was downright awful. No, listen... wait a bit. Then you can tell her they killed me."

"Lucille!" Murana cringed.

"Will you let me *laugh?*"

"Well, okay."

Lucille's eyelids dropped. "Yeah, it's okay. It's okay now, I reckon. Only I got to laugh, Bill."

"I know. Luce?"

"Yeah?"

"You want anything?"

"I got no appetite, honey."

"*Anything*, I meant."

"Wouldn't mind seein' one more Run for the Roses." Lucille's smile was bitter. "To feel hungry'd be fine. To take a bath." Then her expression softened. "I could stand a little more of Roy Beebe's lovin', too. Never could get my fill of that."

"Lucille—"

"Okay, a body can't have everything."

"I know," Murana said. "I know."

Suddenly Lucille's eyes opened, clear and steady. She looked at Murana. "Uncle," she said.

"What?"

"I had enough of this one, Bill." Her fingers tightened around Murana's.

"What are you saying?"

"You know damn well."

Murana pulled her hand away. "No," she said. "I'm saying *no*, you hear? It ain't done yet."

"You say you're my friend . . . do anything in the world for me? I'm asking you. Tell them it's time they let me go."

Murana shook her head, clapping her hands over her ears.

"They could make it easy," Lucille said.

"Not on your life," Murana whispered.

"You said it, honey—*my* life."

Murana stared hard into Lucille's fading blue eyes. "Mine, too," she said. "And you best not forget it."

"The life gone out of me, Bill, a good while back."

"No."

"The pain . . . the stink."

"Like you said, abide."

"The pain and the stink ain't yours. You got no earthly notion what it's like."

"Oh, yes I *do*."

"I want to go," Lucille wept. "Anything else gettin' too hard. Can't you just let me go?"

Murana bent down and grasped her chin. Lucille squeezed her eyes shut. The overcolored face of a clown stared, eyeless, at the shadow-strewn ceiling.

"Look at me. You best look at me, Lucille Beebe."

She wrenched her head free with surprising strength.

Murana brought her lips close to Lucille's ear. "I'm with you," she said. "I'm here."

"Go away," Lucille said. "Go on with you."

. . .

Her eyes remained closed, and she never spoke another word. She was in a coma, the doctors said.

Murana knew better.

For two days and two nights, she didn't leave Lucille's bedside. She took off the jockey costume and put it in the closet, where she found the dress Lucille had worn when she first came to the hospital—a fuchsia silk sheath, sleeveless, with a ruffled neckline. Murana put it on, thinking the two of them could have fit in it together now. The tight boots soon made her feet swell, so she went barefoot. Eventually, one of the nurses found a pair of felt slippers for her to wear, something someone had lost or left behind.

After the first night, Dr. Ahmed, giving up his efforts to get her to go home, ordered a cot to be put in the room. But Murana didn't use it. Even when she slept, which was hardly at all, she did so in the chair, pulled right up alongside the bed. Mr. Beebe came in the afternoon, but finding Murana there, he left in no time, wouldn't even sit in the chair when she offered it to him.

When he moved to go, after staring down at his wife for a few minutes, Murana followed him out into the corridor. "You know . . . it ain't good," she said, touching his arm.

His fawn-colored eyes narrowed like he was angry. "Ain't hardly real," he said. Then he turned and walked off.

The next afternoon, however, he came back, and every afternoon after that. Now he shook Murana's hand when he came into the room. One day he brought her a milk shake. "You look a little washed out," he said.

When her hands weren't occupied tending Lucille, Murana held her rosary beads. But most of the time she couldn't keep her mind on the proper prayers. She'd begin a decade, "Glory be to the Father . . ." Next thing she knew, she'd be speaking to the Lord in her own words. They weren't always respectful, either. "Thy will be done, You say. But where's that famous mercy You's always talkin' about, I'd like to know?"

The one she was really mad at, though, was Lucille. And she figured if she knew it herself, then the Lord likely knew it too. And would forgive her. Much as she tried to concentrate on Heaven, sooner or later it always came back to Lucille.

"You look at me now. You best look at me, Lucille Beebe."

And sometimes, since Lucille wasn't watching anyhow, Murana allowed herself to cry. "Don't leave me this way," she begged.

On the third day, however, Murana faced up to the fact that Lucille had turned from her, had, like Lyman Gene, already gone to a place where Murana couldn't follow.

That afternoon, for the first time, Murana longed to flee from the hospital. It was almost dusk. Lucille was breathing softly, evenly. She never changed position anymore, unless Murana and one of the nurses turned her.

Murana sat in the bedside chair, staring blankly at the large plate-glass window. It was tinted, grayish, so that you couldn't really tell how the sky looked, even when you studied it. Murana felt a craving for air, for the sight of the sky's true color.

Then she imagined a swath of shimmering transparent paper covering her lap and cascading to the floor. It would be the shade of amethysts. Or emeralds, perhaps.

The cellophane undulated and changed color like a mythical sea. Murana could see her own hands, so deft, so delicate, controlling the tides. And the silver shears flew as they dropped a world of wonders among the folds of her skirt: birds and flowers and stars, angels and apostles and ordinary people with houses better than their dreams, long safe streets unknown to want and sorrow . . .

She was making a cellophane window to show Lucille China and Africa, the Rockies and Old Faithful, glories that dulled and defeated Heaven. And when Lucille saw it, she'd be so mad at what she'd be missing that she'd plain *refuse* to die.

A young nurse came into the room and smiled at Murana when she started jumpily awake. Next to Lucille's, the girl's face, as she bent over the bed, seemed astonishingly pink, almost like an artificial flower.

The window was only a dream, Murana realized. It made no sense. Nothing she could do now made any sense, except sitting here, abiding, saying such prayers as she could muster. But a prayer seemed hardly more reliable than a dream.

The nurse studied the chart hanging on the foot rail of the bed for a moment. Then she took Lucille's blood pressure and checked on the tubes feeding her.

"Can you tell me anything?" Murana whispered.

The girl shook her head, looking uneasy.

Murana sighed.

The nurse went out, silent on her rubber soles.

Murana leaned over the edge of the bed, her palms pressed down on the Hosanna Quilt, and brought her lips close to Lucille's ear. "Can you tell me anything?" she repeated.

There was a moment of perfect stillness. Then, very slowly, Lucille's eyes opened. They flickered. Murana holding the poor ruined face between her hands, turned her head to the left, toward the window which framed the ambiguous sky.

Lucille's eyes widened, catching the light, then fluttered closed again.

Ten days later, with everything that could be done, done, Lucille died. It was the supper hour, a crystal, star-scattered evening. The moon rose early. Murana saw it hovering in the window, a disc of colorless light caught in a sheer net of clouds.

EPILOGUE

*O*n a dismal Saturday morning in mid-November, as the U of L football team suited up for the game with Wichita State and Louisville housewives began to give some serious thought to Thanksgiving, a memorial service for Lucille Beebe was held in the blue-and-gold music room at the Pleasant Knoll Home.

All the residents and staff of the Home were there, along with the widower and a young Unitarian chaplain from the hospital, to whom the deceased had taken a decidedly un-theological shine. He was a tall, broad-shouldered blond with silver eyebrows and an engaging smile.

Judge Dudley delivered the eulogy, drawing heavily upon the works of Emerson and the poems of John Greenleaf Whittier, which he had learned by rote as a boy.

Mrs. Kinsella read briefly from the Book of Psalms. Then Mrs. Royce and Miss Lightner, wearing black silk dresses that appeared to be identical, passed among the ladies of Pleasant Knoll, presenting a white rose to each.

Somehow, one flower was left over, its petals not quite open yet. Miss Lightner handed it impulsively to the judge, who was wiping his eyes with a maroon handkerchief that matched his necktie.

"Let us pray," the chaplain said.

When the prayers had ended, the old people glanced around expectantly. It seemed as if there should be something more, some high point not yet come. The chaplain looked bewildered. The widower shifted in his chair and examined his new black shoes.

Finally, however, as some of the residents started to rise from their chairs, a scraping sound came from the back of the room. Two women—one gangly and pale, the other stunted and dark—left their places and approached the piano by the bay window. Behind them, the sky was clogged with pewter-colored clouds and the first hesitant light of clearing.

Sitting at the piano bench, the tiny woman raised her child-sized hands above the keyboard, shaking back her long sleeves. Then she turned and looked questioningly at the second woman, who was standing behind her. The younger woman sighed softly, closing her eyes, then nodded. Like nearly every other woman in the room, she wore a sober black dress. But over it she had on a red jacket whose brass buttons gleamed in the glare from the window.

The woman at the piano waited another second or two, her hands still hovering over the keys. Then she twisted around to take the other woman's wrist and pull her down to sit by her side on the bench.

The larger woman sighed again, opened her eyes, and sat.

Finally, one stubby dark finger, straight and sure, poked the middle C. Deep in her chest, the old woman echoed the note, holding it until her companion began to hum, too.

The tall woman straightened her spine. The small one lifted her face. They looked deep in one another's eyes. And when they smiled, it was as if light had broken in the sky behind them and their voices flooded the room with warmth:

"This little light o' mine..."

And together, they kept right on singing, until everyone in the room had joined in, even Mrs. Kinsella, who wondered privately whether "Amazing Grace" mightn't have been a more fitting choice.

In the music room, the old folks were still lingering over tea sandwiches and cookies. Nobody had much appetite. The refreshments were just something to keep off being alone. Mr. Beebe had disappeared right after the service, though. Deprived of his presence, wanting to express their condolences to someone, the ladies clustered around the chaplain who kept trying to edge toward the door, an anxious expression on his face.

Alone and looking lost, the judge sat backward on the piano bench, a dainty Wedgwood cup balanced on one knee.

Murana wanted sorely to be gone, to get off by herself somewhere. But the sight of the old man's sorrow and confusion drew her to him.

"Judge?"

He looked up, his eyes brimming.

"Are you all right?"

His lower lip trembled like a child's. "There is no justice," he said.

Smiling sadly, Murana bent over and tenderly kissed the top of his head, where the skin was bare and dry and shiny. Then she slipped toward the door, looking back at him again as she went out.

Outside the sun seemed to have come out once and for all. The air was warm. Murana walked down the front steps of the Home and circled around back. There, on a patch of grass beside the kitchen door, she found Mattie.

The old woman was sitting on the ground, her bent legs drawn up to her chin, a ferocious expression on her face. "Don't say nothin'," she said.

"Like what?"

"Like any of yo' damn sweetness and light. I ain't in no mood."

Without looking up, Mattie patted the ground beside her. Murana sat, drawing up her knees.

They sat in silence for a very long time. Occasionally, one of them sighed. Finally, after perhaps a quarter of an hour, Mattie cleared her throat gruffly. "You sang pretty good," she said. "For white folks."

Murana dropped her head, not replying. Her chin rested on her left knee. Another moment went by.

"What the hell," Mattie said. "I guess you might as well go ahead and cry if you want." She scuttled closer and put her arm around Murana's shoulders. It was just barely long enough to span them.

Up above, a breeze shook the topmost branches of a small red maple. They both looked up at the rustling sound. A handful of russet leaves floated down around them. One caught in Mattie's wiry hair. Murana plucked it out and crumbled it in her hand. It fell apart almost like ash.

"Reckon I got time," she said.

Mattie guided Murana's head down to rest against her neck. Her skin smelled like clove. "All the time in the world, child," she said. "Whatever that be."